LIKE A CHRISTMAS DREAM

A PORT WILLIS ROMANCE

LINDSAY HARREL

CHAPTER 1

One fire down, a thousand and one to go.

Sarah Bentley leaned away from her computer and stretched her neck from side to side. How long had she been tucked away in her office with the door closed this morning? Not that she really needed the privacy. All the other in-house counsel for Bentley & Co were spending the day after Thanksgiving with family.

If Sarah really wanted to be with her family, she'd simply take the elevator to the thirty-first floor and find her father in the CEO's massive corner office. Or she could head home and be roped into helping Mother plan their annual Christmas Eve soiree.

No thanks. She'd take pointless, stressful work any day.

Of course, she wouldn't have minded spending the day with her siblings, but Benjamin was likely working too—being vice-president at a Bentley & Co subsidiary was just as demanding as Sarah's position, if not more so—or out for drinks with his friends or flavor-of-the-week girlfriend.

And Ginny . . . well, her younger sister lived halfway around the world, and Sarah hadn't seen her in more than seven years.

Then, out of the blue, last week, Sarah had received that email. An invitation . . .

She sighed and glanced out of her office's large picture window across downtown Boston. Though the snow from earlier had stopped falling, clouds on the horizon threatened a repeat. Instead of glistening like it did in the summertime, the Charles River looked still and somber. And The Pru, a skyscraper that had first made its mark on the Boston skyline in the sixties, appeared much taller, more intimidating, than usual.

The weather matched her mood quite perfectly.

But if she could just work for a few more hours, then maybe she'd be able to fully enjoy her second date with Warren this afternoon.

As Sarah prepared to jump back into the proverbial flames, her cell phone's ringtone pierced the quiet.

She didn't recognize the number, and a little flutter lifted her chest. "Hello?" No one spoke, but ragged breathing filled the line.

Most people would get annoyed at what

appeared to be a crank call, but over the last three years, Sarah had received more calls like this than she could count. She gentled her voice. "Who am I speaking to?"

"S-Sarah?"

Sarah tried to place the woman's voice. Was it Brittany, the young fireman's wife she'd met with last week to discuss her options? But no, the voice sounded more mature than that.

Suddenly, it clicked. "Elise, is that you?"

More silence.

Elise Gentry. Oh, wow. So many implications if this was indeed the woman she thought it was.

So many ways Sarah could help.

So many ways she could fail.

She pushed away from her desk and stood to pace. "Please, tell me how I can help." When she placed her hand against the cold pane, Sarah's palm burned at the contact.

This was the hardest part—being powerless to do anything but wait.

"Yes, it's Elise. And I'm ready. To leave him." A determination rang through the words. "He's never going to touch me again. And I won't give him the chance to hurt Rose. I . . . I have to be strong. For her."

And no matter how many doubts assailed Sarah at the moment, *she* had to be strong for Elise. "Elise, I'm proud of you. I know that cannot have been an easy decision. We can talk more at my office, but first I need to know where you are. Are you safe?"

"Yes. I spent the morning packing. Jeff is out of town on business until next week." An audible gulp. "My s-sister is with me. I'm calling from her phone."

"Good. You've done so well. I can be at my office in fifteen minutes. Are you able to meet me there?"

"I can be there in about forty-five minutes." A pause. "Thank you, Sarah."

Hopefully Elise would still be thanking her in weeks, months, even years from now. "Of course. You know where it is?"

"I do." With every word, the woman sounded a tiny bit stronger, an amazing feat for what Sarah suspected she'd been through.

She had first encountered Elise Gentry at a charity event a year ago. They'd been casually chatting—Sarah telling Elise what she did as an attorney at Bentley & Co, Elise regaling her with details about life being married to one of the city's most prominent businessmen—when Sarah had told her about her *other* job. Her passion project, the one that had first settled in her heart during her nonprofit law class at Yale nearly ten years ago.

Elise's eyes had told Sarah everything she needed to know. But up until now, the woman had never come right out and confirmed Sarah's suspicions.

"See you then. And Elise?"

"Yes?"

"It's going to be okay. We're going to help you." *Please let that be true.*

Sarah hung up, snatched her purse, threw on her coat and scarf, and practically sprinted from her office. Once she made it down the long hallway and the twenty stories to the bottom floor of Bentley & Co's building, it should only take five minutes to walk to the offices of New Dawn Women's Council, a non-profit Sarah had founded with her best friend Melissa. Their organization provided women in abusive relationships free legal counsel in custody and divorce proceedings. They also put them in touch with shelters and other services they might need during the transition period.

Most often, New Dawn helped low-income women who had nowhere else to turn. Occasionally, however, they provided services to women from well-to-do families whose husbands controlled the pursestrings. And them.

But those cases—where judges could be paid off, where the court of public opinion could ruin a wife's reputation thanks to a few well-placed rumors, where money could often buy the best lawyers in town—were much more difficult to win.

And these women, they depended on Sarah. She couldn't afford to let them down.

If only she could give more of herself to New Dawn. But Father still expected twelve-plus-hour workdays at Bentley & Co. She should be grateful that he'd agreed to fund New Dawn in the first place —even if she knew exactly why he'd done it.

After all, Father never did anything without a calculated reason.

No wonder Ginny had run far away from Boston —all the way to England—and not looked back. If only Sarah were that brave.

The wind tousled Sarah's carefully arranged hair and blew against her favorite Michael Kors red ruffle belted wool trench coat as she trudged toward the nonprofit. Despite the fact it was after the lunch hour and threatening to snow again, people jostled for position on the sidewalk. Car horns cursed in short beeps, and vendors hocked their wares from lime green and silver carts that lined the street.

It took Sarah a few minutes longer than usual to reach her destination, but finally, she arrived, stepping inside the building and taking the elevator to the fourth floor. Her Prada heels clicked on the travertine as she entered Office 405, discreetly labeled as NDWC. She bypassed the small but stylish waiting area, waved hello to the receptionist Jackie, and headed to her own office—only a fourth the size of her space at Bentley, but everything she could want or need: a comfy chair, a filing cabinet in the corner, and a mid-sized but well-appointed desk, on which rested a photo of her and Melissa, who ran this place when Sarah couldn't be here. The room still smelled like the lavender essential oil she'd diffused the last time she'd been here, meeting with a client. Today, it did nothing to calm her nerves.

As Sarah peeled off her coat, Melissa popped her head inside the door. "What are you doing here?" Her friend's dark skin and curly hair had always contrasted Sarah's pale complexion and straight auburn locks, and her style was much more casual— as proven by the flannel shirt and faded jeans she currently sported. But in all the ways that mattered, especially regarding New Dawn, the two fell into complete sync.

"Elise Gentry is on her way in."

Melissa's eyes went wide as she moved into the office. In her hands she held a Hershey's kiss, most likely from the giant bowl on her own desk. "Looks like you were right."

"Unfortunately."

The kiss's tiny foil jacket crinkled in Melissa's fingers as she unwrapped the chocolate. "I'll make sure Jackie brings her straight back when she arrives." She slipped the kiss inside her cheek.

Sarah had been so busy considering all the details that she'd forgotten to alert Jackie herself. "Thanks, Mel. You're a gem." Moving to her file cabinet, she slid open the top drawer and pulled a few pamphlets from a folder. The pamphlets would describe what was ahead.

Elise might think that leaving was the hardest part, but winning custody and getting what she deserved—more than deserved—from a man as well connected and respected as Jeff Gentry?

Sarah would be gentle but honest—it was going to be the most difficult thing Elise had ever done.

Maybe Sarah too.

"Hey." Melissa's hand pressed against Sarah's shoulder.

Sarah turned and found her friend's eyes on her, radiating concern.

"You're going to do great."

"Maybe you should take this one." Despite Mel's relaxed exterior, she was a shark in the courtroom. Having been first years together at Yale, they'd been practicing law for the same amount of time. But instead of wasting away in corporate law like Sarah had been forced to do, Melissa had spent her days fighting against child abuse at the Department of Children and Families.

"You've cultivated trust with the client already."

"You know who Jeff Gentry is, though, right?" Sarah closed the drawer a bit more forcefully than she'd intended. The snap reverberated in the room. "Owner of Gentry Pharmaceuticals. Philanthropist. Voted Boston's Mr. Congeniality two years in a row."

"And, apparently, we can add abusive jerk to his resume."

Sarah blew out a breath and tried to quiet the

bees buzzing around in her chest. "Elise deserves the best against a guy like that."

"And who better to give her that than someone who knows that world so well? I'm just a poor kid from Philly. But you . . . you're Sarah Bentley. Of the Boston Bentleys."

Her friend's voice teased, but Sarah wasn't in the mood to deal with thoughts of who everyone assumed she was just because of her family connections. She rolled her eyes as she sat and arranged all the necessary paperwork on her desk.

Melissa plopped into the chair across from her and waited until Sarah looked up. "Look, I know you hate everyone thinking you're this spoiled princess who only got a job at Daddy's firm because of your name—"

"Gee, thanks."

"But obviously, you're someone who deeply cares about others. And you're wicked smart to boot. So stop doubting yourself, get inside this case, and do what you do best. Advocate."

"I just wish I could be here more, you know? Give more of myself to this."

Melissa arched an eyebrow. "Whenever you feel like standing up to Daddy dearest, you know I'm behind you one thousand percent."

"It's not that simple. The moment I do, we're out of funding." Sarah snapped her fingers. "Just like that."

"We'd figure it out."

"And in the meantime, women and children would suffer while we waited for donors to come through. I'll just have to work harder."

"You're already running yourself into the ground. Maybe what you actually need is a vacation. Have you thought of that?"

"Bentleys don't take vacations. Not real ones, anyway."

"You know, bringing work with you kind of defeats the purpose of a vacation."

"Exactly. There's no escape."

"What about your sister's bakery thing? You could reconnect with her and get a vacation out of it. Bam. Two birds. I can help cover this case while you're out."

"The only thing Father would hate more than allowing me time away from work would be me visiting Ginny."

To her parents, Ginny Bentley Rose had been all but disowned when she'd dropped out of school, followed a Brit to a tiny village in Cornwall, and married him at the age of twenty-one. A few years ago, he'd divorced her, but instead of falling apart and coming home, according to her social media accounts—which, yes, Sarah followed—Ginny had gone to culinary school in London. Now she was back in Port Willis and opening her own bakery just before Christmas.

And even though her family had scorned Ginny, she had extended a peace offering in the form of an invitation to her grand opening.

Part of Sarah longed to go . . . but the rest of her knew how impossible it would be.

Not that it mattered what Sarah wanted. It never had, not to her parents, especially her father. The only thing he'd ever caved on was allowing her to open New Dawn—but in order to do it, she'd had to promise never to leave Bentley & Co.

And, as the oldest child, to eventually replace her father as CEO.

When you were a Bentley, everything came with a price.

"Why do you give in to him?" Melissa's voice was tinged with frustration.

"Because I've seen what happens when people defy him." Father'd always had a soft spot for Ginny, his youngest, but when she'd rebelled, he hadn't hesitated to cut her out of his life—not just out of his will, but out of his heart too.

As much as Sarah despised his way of doing things, he was still her father. The only one she had. If she was nothing to him, then who was she to everyone else?

That's why New Dawn was so important. It was the only thing that made Sarah feel like herself. Or at least, the person she wanted to be.

Straightening her spine, Sarah adjusted her

blouse. Elise would be here any moment. Time to focus. Time to fake the confidence she had to feel in order to tackle this case and win it. Not only for Elise and women everywhere just like her.

But also, for Sarah herself.

IF SARAH HAD WRITTEN the perfect man into existence, he would probably look and act a lot like Warren Kensington.

Warren put his BMW into Park in front of her parents' home and studied Sarah from behind his thick black frames. "I had a really nice time with you this afternoon."

Sarah fidgeted with the strap of her purse. "Me too." And she had. After pulling herself together enough to take the meeting with Elise Gentry, she'd needed a distraction, and Warren had provided it in spades. He wasn't just handsome to look at, with his nary-a-lock-out-of-place tapered haircut, his piercing brown eyes, his square jawline, and impeccable style in clothing. Warren also possessed a true kindness in his spirit, something that Sarah hadn't seen in a man she'd dated in a very long time.

That was what happened when she went out with guys from her circle, which was why Warren had surprised her. She might not feel tingles up her spine when he held her hand, but they got along well.

And best of all, her father had nothing to do with her decision to date him.

"I'd better let you get inside." Despite his words, the wistfulness in Warren's eyes told her it was the last thing he wanted to do.

"Yeah, I shouldn't be late for dinner. Mother will never forgive me if the food that Betsy made gets cold." Sarah quirked one side of her lips. "I mean . . . talk about tragedy."

A smile flitted across Warren's lips. "I won't be party to that for sure." Tentatively, he lifted a hand and swept a strand of hair back from Sarah's face, his finger tracing a line down her cheek. Was he thinking about kissing her? Did she want him to? It had been so long since she'd really been kissed. Working crazy long hours didn't leave much room for a social life. "When can I see you again?"

"I'd love to say soon, but I'm just not sure." As a look of doubt crossed Warren's features, she rushed to reassure him. "I mean it. I've got so many projects. Even if I work from now until New Year's, I won't complete half of them. And then there's New Dawn . . ." Her initial meeting with Elise had gone well enough, and they planned to meet again on Sunday once her new client had time to get settled at her sister's house and gather some documents.

"I admire the work you do there so much."

If only Mother and Father could see it the way Warren did. "Thank you."

Her phone buzzed from her purse. A quick glance showed Mother's name on the screen. "That's my cue." Sarah reached for the door handle.

"Here, let me get that." Racing around to her door, Warren popped it open and gave her a hand. A breezy chill hit her legs, and her heels crunched on the snow left over from this morning's storm as she climbed out.

She looked up into Warren's eyes. "Thanks again for a great time." It may have only been cappuccinos and pastries at her favorite bakery, but the conversation had been just as pleasant as the treats. "I'll text you when I get an opening in my schedule."

"I'll be waiting." His gaze drifted momentarily to her mouth, then back to her eyes, and before she knew what was happening, he had met her lips with his. The kiss was brief, but nice.

As Warren straightened again, Sarah smiled. "I'm glad you finally asked me out."

The Kensingtons and Bentleys had been friends for ages—having met during summers spent in Nantucket—but Warren had only ever been friends with Benjamin, who was two years younger than Sarah. Earlier this year, Warren had taken over the Boston branch of Kensington Corporation, a multi-faceted organization based in New York that specialized in everything from technology to pharmaceuticals. Sarah and Warren had reconnected at a charity event to raise money for victims of domestic violence.

"Me too. I was surprised when your father suggested it, but—"

"What, wait?"

Warren scratched behind his ear. "Your dad and mine have been meeting at least once a month for a while now. I thought you knew. During one of his visits to our offices, he mentioned that you were single and looking to . . ." His cheeks reddened. "Anyway, I'd always thought you were beautiful, but figured I didn't stand a chance with you."

The blood pumped faster through Sarah's veins. "My father set us up?"

"I wouldn't say *set us up*, but—"

"I can't believe this." Did he think he had a say in every area of her life? First, where she'd go to college, then what she'd major in, then where she'd work after college, then where she'd spend her career. And now he was trying to interfere in her love life too?

"I didn't mean to upset you."

Sarah exhaled through the tightness in her chest. It wasn't Warren's fault he'd been a pawn in George Bentley's machinations.

He had a reason for every move he made. This wouldn't be an exception.

Wait. "You said he's been meeting with your dad regularly?"

Warren nodded. "I think they're in early discussions about a merger."

Of course they were. Sarah ran a gloved hand across her forehead where a headache had started to form. "Thanks for the information." She cringed at the cold, informal tone of her voice—but at the moment, she couldn't muster any warmth.

Was she overreacting? Probably. Still, she couldn't stop the tremble that shook her hands as she gripped her purse.

Her parents could have her career in exchange for their affection. Fine.

They might be able to coerce her into following their intended trajectory for her life.

But they could not have her love life. No matter how many times she'd backed down on what she wanted in the past, she wasn't giving *that* up without a fight. "I need to go."

"Have I screwed everything up?" Warren looked miserable, his brow knit in confusion, lips pushed to one side.

She reached out a hand and touched his arm gently. "No, it's just—" Words fled her brain, and Sarah simply squeezed. "I need to get inside. I'll . . . text you."

Turning on her heel, she strode from the circular brick driveway toward the massive front door of the hilltop Georgian manor in Boston's Metro West suburbs. Stepping inside the home where she'd lived all her life, warmth enveloped Sarah—warmth that had nothing to do with the people who lived here, but rather the fact that a fireplace near the entrance roared and crackled.

Since she'd left for work this morning, the servants had decked the grand entrance with Christmas decor. A sixteen-foot Christmas tree sparkled with lights and gorgeous designer ornaments from all over the world. Garland circled the banister of the curving wooden staircase, and the mantel of the fireplace in the front sitting room displayed a fancy Advent calendar that had delighted Sarah as a child—that is, until her mother had caught her sneaking chocolate and paddled her so hard that even seeing the calendar now made her backside ache with phantom pain.

As Sarah shrugged out of her coat and scarf, one of the maids raced around the corner. "I'm so sorry for not being here when you arrived, Ms. Bentley." She took Sarah's things before Sarah could allay her concern, and took off toward the coat closet.

Sarah steeled herself for the dinner ahead. Still sorting through her feelings about Warren, she walked toward the formal dining room.

Mariah Bentley sat at one end of the table, George Bentley at the other—a queen and king presiding over their subjects, aka Benjamin and now Sarah. Salads adorned each of their plates, but no one was eating.

Mother's head snapped to attention the moment Sarah set foot into the room. "Nice of you to finally join us." Her regal attire tonight consisted of a red long-sleeved blouse that fluttered from shoulder to wrist and black Dolce & Gabbana slacks that complemented her trim figure. Even her hair—sleeked back in a brown-and-no-trace-of-gray bob—seemed perfectly suited for a crown.

"You could have started without me." The words popped out, surprising no one more than her. She never talked back to her parents. But with Warren's revelation, something unusual had lit inside of her, burning her gut.

Mother recovered quickly, though one eyebrow remained arched. "*We* didn't want to be rude."

Sarah pursed her lips together and slid into a chair across from Benjamin, catching the amused look in his eyes. She'd kick him but her legs didn't reach underneath the sixteen-person table. "I was simply saying good-bye to Warren."

Now that she knew his motives, it wasn't hard to catch the quirk of a smile on Father's lips. "I suppose we can forgive her then, can't we, Mariah?" He forked a cucumber with his fork and put it to his thick lips. At age fifty-five, George Bentley struck an imposing figure with his full head of salt-and-pepper hair and six-foot-four frame. Though slightly rotund around the waist, her mother's efforts to stave off his diabetes had been largely successful.

He'd discarded his Armani suit jacket but still wore his yellow shirt and black tie, and his Rolex winked from beneath his left cuff.

Snatching her cloth napkin from the table, Sarah fluffed it onto her lap. "I won't be seeing him again." She could feel Mother's sharp gaze boring into her, but picked up her fork and shoved some salad into her mouth anyway. The bite of garlic in the dressing took her by surprise, and she forced a swallow.

"And why is that?" How was it possible for Father's voice to boom across the room louder than usual?

Sarah straightened her spine, but refused to look at either of her parents. "Because I draw the line at an arranged marriage."

Benjamin guffawed across the table, and Sarah speared him with a glare that left his bright blue eyes laughing. He ran a hand through a textured crop of brown hair that had always made his sisters envious.

"Excuse me?"

Sarah's gaze flitted to Father. "I know you suggested he ask me out. I'm assuming it's because you're considering a merger with his family and want an 'in,' but *I* want no part of that." Oh goodness. When was the last time she'd spoken this way to him? Her insides trembled as she stabbed a cherry tomato with her fork, and the juices oozed out onto the lettuce underneath.

"You're clearly overreacting, dear."

"No, Mariah, she's right. I do think it'd go a long way in Scott's mind. You know how family-oriented he is." His words twisted at the end, as if they represented something odious.

So he wasn't even going to deny it. Maybe he had a shred of respect for her after all. "I have no interest in using Warren to make your goals come to fruition." What was wrong with her? Why couldn't she stop the flow of anger spewing from her lips?

The mutilated tomato slid into her mouth and she choked it down with a gulp of water.

Silence filled the room for a full minute before her father spoke again. "I think you should reconsider."

Of course he did.

Sarah looked to Benjamin, her only potential ally in the room. With her eyes, she pleaded with him to change the subject.

"So, how about that invite from Ginny, huh? Will you be going, Mother? Father?" Her brother's eyes twinkled.

Troublemaker.

Sarah stuffed more food into her mouth and peeked at Mother from the corner of her eyes.

Mother's pursed lips pulled her whole face taut. "It's ridiculous—opening a bakery just before Christmas Eve. She's losing out on an entire holiday season's worth of profits. And to think she went to Harvard business school . . ."

"Soooo, you're not going then?"

"No, Benjamin, of course not. You know we have our annual Christmas Eve party."

Nice excuse—as if they'd have gone otherwise. No, Ginny had been disowned, and for what? Daring to follow her heart?

The subject changed and the family descended into inane conversation—and with each moment, Sarah's chest grew tighter. Who were these people to try to dictate their children's every move? Didn't they have a right to their own lives?

But no, Father had always ruled his household with a firm fist and sound "logic." And Sarah had let him. Not since she was thirteen years old had she truly rebelled against anything he'd asked of her— until now. And suddenly, refusing to date Warren didn't seem like enough.

Maybe in order to break free, to show her parents that she was her own person, Sarah needed to make an even bigger stand. Who knew? Perhaps they'd even respect her for it.

"The only thing Father would hate more than allowing me time away from work would be me visiting Ginny." Sarah's own words from earlier today floated back to her.

What if . . . was it completely crazy?

Before she could really consider all the ramifications of her idea, Sarah's mouth betrayed her once again. "I'm planning to go to England for a few weeks. For Ginny's bakery opening."

Mother's fork clattered to her plate, and one glance at Father proved she'd been delusional to think he might ever respect her for being her own person. The tips of his ears were turning red. He placed his fork on his plate, pushed it away, and folded his hands on the table, staring Sarah down.

She swallowed hard.

At last, he nodded. "Fine."

Huh? "Fine?"

"Yes, fine. I'll grant you the leave. You can represent our family and bring back news of Ginny's endeavors. If you'd like, you can bring work with you. Better yet, I'll hire someone temporarily to take on some of your projects. And why only go for such a short time? Take the whole month. Leave this week."

This week? Could she really do that? Her head spun with the details. She'd need to talk to Melissa about whether she could handle everything at New Dawn, especially with Elise's case, but her friend had sat in on the initial meeting and was as aware as Sarah for now. Besides, legal proceedings usually slowed down in the month of December anyway . . .

And then there was the chance to reconnect with Ginny. More time meant more reconnection. Of course, it also granted more time for awkwardness and pain between them.

Her gaze narrowed. "What's the catch?" There was always a catch.

"You may go, but you must be back for your mother's Christmas Eve party. With the time difference, that means that you should be able to leave directly after the grand opening and return in time."

It would be tight, but Sarah would make it work. "Done."

"And"—the light from the chandelier above them caught a gleam in Father's eyes—"you will attend the party with Warren Kensington."

So that's what he was playing at. Well, fine. She could attend one party with him. That didn't mean she was going to continue to date him. And it's not like she despised his company.

Sarah fisted the napkin in her lap and ground out a reply. "All right." The legs of her chair screeched against the polished wood as she stood abruptly. "Guess I'd better get packing."

CHAPTER 2

*I*t had been three—no four—days, but Sarah had finally arrived in the small Cornish fishing village known as Port Willis.

"I can drop you at the car park or harbor, miss. Which do you prefer?" The chauffeur she'd hired at the Cornwall Airport Newquay watched her from his rearview mirror as he idled, waiting for her answer.

"Do you know where the local bookstore is?" Sarah didn't know much about Ginny's new life, but she did know that the soon-to-open bakery was somehow connected to the bookstore she used to own with her ex-husband Garrett. According to the bookstore's website, a woman named Sophia Rose was the bookstore's current owner. "My phone is dead or I'd look it up on GPS." How she'd managed to forget her charging cord was anyone's guess. Might have been the nerves threatening to take over whenever she thought about being reunited with her sister.

"Sorry, miss. My reception isn't what I'd like. I need a new phone myself." The sixty-something man's eyes twinkled underneath his bushy gray eyebrows.

"No worries. The harbor is fine. I'm sure I can find someone to help."

People strolled along the small sidewalks past storefronts that looked to be something out of a Robert Appleton novel. Even from within the vehicle, she could feel the history in this place thrumming, a living, ever-evolving thing. Through the car doors, Sarah caught whiffs of a variety of smells all swirling together as they passed a fudge shop, a bakery, and several pubs. Raucous laughter greeted her ears as they drove by a restaurant with big windows revealing walls lined with televisions broadcasting some kind of sport.

The sun was just setting over the water as the car approached the harbor, where a handful of sailboats and dinghies bobbed.

"Here we are." The car rolled to a stop in front of a restaurant.

Sarah leaned closer to the window and made out the restaurant's name on its weathered blue sign. "The Village Pub."

"Might grab myself a nice warm supper before I head back out. Would you care to join me?"

"Oh." She'd murmured the words to herself, not expecting a reply. "That's very kind, but I need to find my sister. She lives here."

"And she didn't arrange to pick you up from the airport herself? It's only a half hour's drive."

"She doesn't know I'm coming."

"Ah, a surprise visit. That sounds lovely." The man clambered from the car and popped the trunk to the four-door sedan.

Sarah scrubbed a hand across her face. It would be a surprise, all right. Lovely? One could only hope.

But after seven years of nearly radio silence between them . . . Well, it might not be a bad idea for Sarah to get a room at the local inn, just in case Ginny's welcome was not as warm as the invitation to her bakery's opening had seemed. For all Sarah knew, Ginny had been inviting her family out of spite—to show them that she'd done what they'd all doubted she could do.

Follow her dreams and actually succeed.

The chauffeur opened Sarah's door and greeted her with a cheery smile. "Here you go, miss."

"Thank you." She took his offered hand and stepped from the vehicle. Her eyes trekked up the hill. Oops. The four-inch pumps she wore may have been her go-to for business dealings and airport travel, but they would make traversing the cobblestone street under her feet fairly challenging. At least the rest of her was properly attired with her scarf, gloves, and parka. A quick glimpse at the weather forecast a few days ago had shown an average of forty degrees, and while snow wasn't overly common in December, it did happen on occasion. But after the bitter cold snap Boston had just experienced, this was nothing.

She paid the man his tip and snagged her rolling suitcase from him. As he disappeared inside the pub, she took the opportunity to finally be alone and get her bearings. There were many lit windows down here by the water, but most seemed to be private residences. The street where she stood—appropriately labeled High Street, according to the adorable wrought-iron streetlamp—ended at the harbor and cut through the middle of town, rising, rising, rising, until it curved away from her eyes.

As she faced the harbor, Sarah got the sudden urge to climb aboard one of the boats and sail away. A breeze tickled her nose and sent strands of hair skimming across her lips. She closed her eyes and inhaled the briny air. *Courage*, it seemed to whisper. Or maybe that was her own heart, begging.

"If I had my camera with me, you'd make a pretty picture indeed."

Sarah whirled, finding a well-built man with a mop of brown curls and cable-knit sweater standing outside the pub, hands shoved into the pockets of his worn jeans. There was something so casual and self-assured about his stance, and the smile on his face only added to his small-town charm.

Of course, the way the British accent glided from his lips didn't hurt his appeal either.

And here Sarah was, gaping like a wide-mouthed fish. She straightened. "Excuse me?" The words came out sharper than she'd intended.

"I'm sorry, didn't mean to startle you." He moved a step closer and glanced at her suitcase. "We don't get many visitors in the winter months. Certainly not as many as in the summer."

"Right." She swallowed a lump that had formed in her throat. How was it possible she could stare down sharks in the courtroom, but this man she'd laid eyes on moments ago flustered her? "I'm visiting my sister, Ginny Bentley—I mean Rose. The trouble is, I'm not quite sure where to find her."

"Oh, I know Ginny. Of course, in Port Willis it's difficult to not know everyone, especially when you've grown up here." The man's easy grin unlocked a certain brightness in his eyes—which, if she were looking, she'd have to admit were the most gorgeous seafoam green color she'd ever seen.

Good thing she wasn't looking.

"Would you mind telling me where I can find her?"

"I'll do you one better. I can take you there."

She shifted, her feet pinching in the toes of her

heels. "Thank you, but you can just tell me how to get there."

"It's no trouble. Actually, I've been meaning to pop in to discuss some food photography for the bakery anyway."

His comment earlier about a camera made sense now. "You're a photographer?"

He shrugged. "Professionally, only on the weekends. The rest of the time, I work at the pub." He gestured behind him. "My family owns it."

Sarah peered inside the windows of the Village Pub. Though it was only five o'clock on a Tuesday evening, the bright interior appeared fairly well filled. A fire roared in one corner, and from her vantage point, Sarah could make out a long wooden paddle and anchor hanging on the wall. "It's adorable."

"I'll tell my mother you appreciate her decor."

Sarah gripped the handle of her suitcase. "Please do. And forgive me, but I didn't catch your name."

The man stared at her for a moment before breaking into another grin. "Michael Hammett at your service."

"Sarah Bentley." She held out her hand as she would when making anyone's acquaintance.

But when he reached out, and his large hands enveloped hers, she couldn't help but think she should have allowed a breach in etiquette just this once. She shivered despite the glove that kept her from actually touching his skin.

"Very nice to meet you, Sarah. But I'm an idiot for making you stand here in the cold. Want to make our way to the bookstore?" He turned toward the steep road.

High Street, indeed. Sarah pictured snapping an ankle in her ridiculous shoes and grimaced. But it was too late to turn back now.

For the first time, he eyed her shoes. "It's not far, but I'm happy to get my car and drive you if you'd like."

"That won't be necessary. Just lead the way."

"At least let me take that for you." Before she could protest, he snatched the suitcase gently from her fingers.

"Thank you." They began the uphill trudge, and soon, Sarah's breaths came in short puffs, her toes burning. But at least she hadn't fallen. Yet.

Beside her, Michael struck an impressive figure against the night sky, where thousands of stars twinkled above them. Had she ever seen this many stars at once? Maybe at their Nantucket home, but she'd been too busy going and doing to notice.

At a break in the buildings, the cliffside opened up to a view of rolling grassy hills and a distant lighthouse that appeared to be guarding the little village nestled into the bluffs.

"Ginny doesn't know you're coming, does she?"

The abrupt question made Sarah stumble. In an instant, Michael was grasping her forearm, his hold supportive but not restrictive. Sarah couldn't help being drawn into his worried gaze. Up close, she could see a slight sheen of stubble dotting his cheeks.

"Are you all right?"

What must this man think of her, falling all over herself—and him? Sarah pulled away from his gentle grasp and forced a smile. "Thanks. I clearly wasn't planning for such a hike in these shoes."

He chuckled. "I guess you weren't."

They continued the climb, passing a few others. But the street was fairly deserted. Perhaps this was one of those small towns that mostly shut down at dusk when it wasn't tourist season.

Sarah assessed her words before speaking. "How did you know?"

"Most people don't wear heels around here."

"Not that." Sarah cleared her throat. "That Ginny doesn't know I'm here."

"Ah. Simply because Ginny isn't one for secrets and she hasn't mentioned her family coming. Considering none of us has met any of you, well . . ." He shrugged. "There would be lots of excited chatter spilling from her, I imagine."

Memories of her sister and her "chatter" warmed Sarah's chest. "She is the most genuine person I know." And yet, Father and Mother had never seen it that way. They'd tried their best to change Ginny—to make her "more like Sarah."

She was relieved to know their efforts had been in vain.

"Here we go." Michael pointed across the street to a building that looked to be hundreds of years old—essentially like everything else in this town. Several shops lined the storefront, but the bright yellow door and the sign above it indicated which was the bookstore. The store next to Rosebud Books looked to be undergoing construction.

Sarah crossed the road and read the sign in the window: *Coming Soon: Once Upon a Time Bakery*. Her fingers twitched as she traced the letters.

Michael joined her, shielding his eyes to look inside. "Doesn't seem like anyone is here. Maybe they're at Gin's home. It's just around the corner." He led her to a quaint little cottage.

Her feet ached at this point, but not as much as her heart. Would Ginny be happy to see her, or throw her out on her ear?

Only one way to find out.

She reached out and knocked on the cottage door. The wind snickered around her as she waited. Maybe Michael sensed her anxiety, because he remained silent.

Low voices floated from inside, and finally, the door creaked open.

The woman on the other side of the door was tall

and slender, with stick-straight hair just past her shoulders and warm chocolate eyes that were older and wiser than the ones Sarah had known so well. Her jeans and Beach Boys T-shirt were dusted with flour, her feet bare.

And tears streaked Ginny's cheeks.

A redheaded man sidled up next to Ginny, slipping his arm around her shoulders. His face brightened when he saw Michael. "Hey, mate. Who's this you have with you?"

"Sarah?" The name burbled from Ginny's throat, a mix of astonishment and joy—or so Sarah hoped.

"Hey, Gin." Sarah chewed her bottom lip. "It's good to see you."

CHAPTER 3

In many ways, it was as if the last seven years had never happened.

Sarah sat on Ginny's worn couch as her sister banged around in the kitchen. It was just the two of them in the tiny house. After an awkward hug and round of introductions, Steven—the redhead—and Michael had left the women to chat.

Ginny hadn't said much, had simply taken Sarah's luggage and wheeled it back to her guest room, then told Sarah she could sit while Ginny prepared some tea.

The kitchen sat adjacent to the living room, so Sarah caught glimpses of her sister bobbing in and out of view as she pulled things from cabinets and talked to herself. Meanwhile, she nestled into the couch—such a bright yellow that their mother would surely cringe at the sight of it. The thought made Sarah smile. *Good for you, Gin.*

Boxes filled the room, most without labels. An undecorated Christmas tree stood in the corner by a window that gave a lovely view of the street.

"I've been too busy to decorate it." Ginny balanced two mugs as she padded across the rug.

"What?"

Her sister deposited one of the mugs into Sarah's waiting hands, and Sarah murmured her thanks.

"The tree. One of those boxes—I'm not sure which at the moment—has all of my Christmas decorations and ornaments, but I've been much too wrapped up in moving back from London to Port Willis and getting the bakery ready to open. Steven put up the tree for me, but I just haven't found a spare moment."

And here Sarah was, taking up precious time. Hopefully she could make up for it over the next three and a half weeks by lending her assistance. Not that she was an expert in opening a business by any means. Melissa had done much of the initial setup for New Dawn. But surely she could find some way to help, even if it were manual labor.

"Be right back." Ginny was gone only minutes before she returned with a platter of chocolate chip cookies, which she placed on the coffee table in front of the couch. "These are fresh out of the oven as of an hour ago."

Sarah hadn't had her sister's sweets in so long. Memories of them playing in their large kitchen at home assailed her. The cook used to swat them out if she were there, so Sarah and Gin would sneak back in the evening. That's when Ginny practiced her baking skills—and Sarah showed her support by eating them.

She took a cookie and bit into it, moaning as the heavenly decadence hit her tongue. "Wow. You've gotten even better, if that's possible."

"Well, I did go to culinary school." Ginny's tone betrayed her amusement.

"Right." Sarah polished off the cookie and took a sip of her tea. "Mmm, did you add cream to this?"

"I did. You're drinking that the true British way."

"Nice." Sarah placed both hands around the mug, soaking in its warmth.

Silence settled between them as they both sipped their drinks. Finally, Ginny tilted her head and worried her bottom lip. "So, you just in the neighborhood, or . . .?"

Nerves rattled in Sarah's stomach. She swallowed. "I wanted to come to support you. I can stay till the twenty-third."

"Does that mean you'll be here for the opening?" Her sister's questioning eyes bore into Sarah.

"My return flight is that evening, but yes, that's the plan. If it's okay with you. I can always stay at a hotel." Sarah averted her gaze.

"Of course you're not staying at a hotel. That's as ridiculous as . . . well, serving grilled cheese with chocolate chips."

"Really, Gin?"

"I'm just saying." A pause. "But I must admit, I'm surprised Dad let you come."

Gripping the mug handle, Sarah stood and paced. "I didn't give him much of a choice. He just . . ." She blew out a breath and walked to the window. Outside, a streetlamp burned a beacon into the starry night, illuminating a wooden bench below it. The sight filled her with calm. Here, the Bentleys seemed so far away, as did the life they had planned for her.

Suddenly, Ginny was beside her, sliding her arm through Sarah's. "I know."

The quiet way she said it . . . she *did* know.

But enough about Sarah.

The band around her lungs finally began to ease. If Ginny held any sort of grudge for Sarah's silence over the last seven years, it wasn't apparent. But how could she let it go?

"So how are you, Gin?" *I've missed you.* Why couldn't she say the words? Sarah extricated her arm gently and moved back to the couch.

Her sister stayed at the window a moment longer, then turned and smiled that kid-on-Christmas-morning grin that lit her whole face. "I'm good. Really good." She snagged a cookie from the platter and sank onto the cushions. "Life isn't perfect, but God's blessed me with so much."

Since when did her sister believe in God? They'd grown up with wishy-washy religion, going to church whenever it made their parents look good. Easter, Christmas, that sort of thing.

Of course, there had been those few short years in her teens when Sarah had snuck away to youth group with her friend Rachel. There, she'd found an acceptance she'd been yearning for all her life. But Father had beaten that fledging faith out of her little by little a long time ago. *"It only makes you weak to believe in someone other than yourself."*

Clearly, Ginny's experience had been different. Maybe Sarah would ask her about it sometime.

She cleared her throat. "I'm really proud of you for attending culinary school and opening a bakery. That was always your dream." Even when their parents laughed at her, as if the idea was truly so out of the question.

"Thanks, Sarah. That means a lot." Ginny chewed, her face relaxed as she studied her sister. "It means a lot you're here too. I still can't believe it."

"Yes, well." *I should have come sooner.* "So, Steven . . . he looks to be more than a friend?"

A blush attacked Ginny's cheeks and she swatted at some flyaway strands of her hair. "Yeah, for about a year now. Well, we've been dating a year. Before that, he was a friend, then kind of more than a friend, but I wasn't ready to date anyway for a while after Garrett and I divorced, and . . ." She bit her lip. "I'm rambling. Sorry, I do that sometimes."

Sarah laughed. "You don't think I remember? Mother used to scold you all the time."

"My one great weakness." Ginny stuck her tongue out. "Along with fidgeting, daydreaming, somehow always dirtying my clothes . . ."

"I'm sorry about you and Garrett."

"Thank you. It was definitely a difficult season in my life, but I grew a lot from it. Learned a lot too. About the way I see myself. About the real meaning of success. And about God too."

There it was again—God—sliding right off Ginny's tongue as natural as could be.

Sarah studied her sister. Ginny had always wilted under other people's censure and bloomed under praise. Now that she considered it, the idea of Ginny being able to laugh at all the things their mother had found "wrong" with her was really quite incredible.

She was the older sister, but maybe Sarah could learn a thing or two from Ginny.

"From our brief interaction, Steven seems really nice." Sarah's fingers drummed along the ceramic mug. "How is everything going with the bakery?"

A shadow flitted across Ginny's face. "Mostly well. We've hit a few snags with deliveries and such. Delays in getting my industrial ovens installed, that sort of thing. But we are still on schedule to open. Only . . ." Her smile dimmed.

"What?" Sarah leaned forward slightly.

"Just before you got here, I received a letter. It was tacked to my bakery's front door." Ginny set the mug down and stood to snag an envelope off the mantel.

"And? What does it say?"

"That apparently there's some parish law that says competing businesses can't be opened within a kilometer of each other." Ginny's finger slid along the edge of the envelope as she stared absently at the bare Christmas tree in her living room.

"Can I see it?" Sarah put her mug on the coffee table and held out her hand.

Ginny shrugged and handed it over, then fiddled with the tree branches while Sarah looked over the bundle of papers. Sure enough, someone had printed out a copy of the local code of ordinances. Several pages in, a thick black marker had circled a specific code referencing business regulations within the parish. Sarah skimmed the regulation and her attorney's brain went to work.

She glanced up, gripping the paper in her fist. "Why would someone send you this?"

"I guess I'm in violation of an ordinance I wasn't even aware of." Ginny sank onto the couch, her head in her hand.

"How?"

"Trengrouse Bakery is less than a kilometer away."

Sarah raised an eyebrow. "I passed that on the way here. You're opening a bakery with clear competition so close?"

Ginny pushed her hair from her eyes and sat up straighter. "I'm not dumb."

"I didn't say you were."

"You're right." Her voice softened. "I'm sorry."

The last thing in the world Ginny should be doing was apologizing to Sarah, even if she *had* snapped at her. Not only was the possibility of losing her dream bakery understandably upsetting, but Sarah's seven-year absence from Ginny's life made Sarah the sister with far more to be sorry for. "So what's going on?"

"Mr. Trengrouse has been in business forever, and I didn't want to step on any toes, so I paid him a visit. When I asked him his thoughts on me opening a bakery, he almost seemed relieved. He said he had been considering retirement for a while now, but didn't want to leave the town without a bakery."

"Did he change his mind or something?"

"His daughter Rebecca took over for him about three months ago. She grew up here, but moved away for university or something. I don't really know her, to be honest. I figured she was coming in to help out while her dad closed up shop, but maybe she changed his mind."

"Don't panic. I'll take a look at this and try to get it sorted out. I'm sure there's a loophole." Sarah winked, attempting to feign more confidence than she felt. "There's always a loophole." Sure, she didn't know British law that well, but she was a Bentley, right? Bentleys got things done, no matter what.

Maybe *this* was how Sarah could make up for the past seven years. The idea settled into her heart and warmed her.

Jaw slack, Ginny stared at her. Then, without warning, she jumped forward to hug Sarah around the neck.

It took a few moments before the shock wore off and Sarah hugged her sister back.

CHAPTER 4

Two days into her investigation about the code in question, and Sarah still didn't have any answers for Ginny.

She groaned and shoved her laptop away from her.

"Bad day?"

At the sound of the masculine British accent, her head swiveled to the door of Ginny's cottage. Michael stood in the doorway, a brown vintage leather jacket worn open over a henley sweater, a camera bag slung over his shoulder.

Whew. She'd never found "casual" so attractive.

"Hi. Nice to see you again." Why did she have to sound so formal, as if preparing to take a deposition?

"Sorry to let myself in, but I knocked and no one answered."

"In most places, that would be considered

breaking and entering." She tried to infuse teasing into her voice, but it came out stilted and almost accusatory.

And there was that infuriatingly crooked-yet-perfect grin again, the one that had melted her defenses on Tuesday when they'd first met. "Ah, but you're in Port Willis now, and that means you can enter when your friend is expecting you and doesn't answer. Most would consider it a politeness, to make sure that friend is in fact all right and not in dire straits."

Sarah slid from the stool that sat under the granite countertop bar of Ginny's kitchen and ran a hand down the red tunic covering her black leggings. With her hair pulled back in a bun and her oversized reading glasses pushed high on her nose, she wasn't exactly dressed for company. "I wasn't aware I was expecting you." She removed the glasses and placed them on the counter.

Michael closed the door behind him and came closer, his smile held in place. For goodness's sake—how had she not noticed those dimples before? But it had been dark last time. "I meant your sister. She asked me to take some photos for her website, remember?"

"Oh. Right." That made sense. Ginny had been baking up a storm since yesterday morning, filling platters with an assortment of cookies, muffins, and other pastries. The kitchen still smelled of cinnamon and nutmeg. She must have been preparing for the shoot.

Of course, Ginny being Ginny, she'd used the opportunity to ply Sarah with sweets—and to try to get her to open up about her life. But what right did Sarah have to drown Ginny in her sorrows when she'd not been there to hear her sister's over the years? So, she'd stuck with the safest of topics: work, particularly the work she was doing at New Dawn. Her sister had been so incredibly supportive of her dream.

When she'd asked if Sarah planned to do it full time someday, Sarah had changed the subject. Of course, she'd wanted to ask Ginny how she'd been so brave as to leave. But leaving wasn't the answer, not for her. It couldn't be or New Dawn wouldn't survive.

"Is she here, then?"

And there Sarah had gone, staring off into space, thinking of how nice it had been to connect with Ginny, to hear her hopes and dreams for the bakery and her future with Steven. Michael must think Sarah a dunce for her inability to focus. "She's at the bakery right now. I can shoot her a text to see if she's coming back, if you'd like."

"Nah, that's all right. It's around the corner, remember? I'll just head over there." He cocked his head. "You *have* seen it, right?"

"Yes, you pointed it out when I arrived." Sarah

picked at a fingernail that she'd worn down to the nub. Mother always fussed at her whenever she went more than a few weeks without a manicure, but there hadn't been time before she came here.

"But surely you've been inside? I figured you'd come early to help her get everything ready."

"I haven't toured it yet." Sarah closed the lid of her laptop and snatched it off the table. "And I'm helping in other ways. Now, if you'll excuse me, I need to get back to it." Turning on her heel, she started toward the guest room, but Michael was in front of her in an instant, blocking her way.

"I'm sorry if I offended you."

The contrition in his voice brought her attention to him. Mistake. From here she could see flecks of gold in his eyes. That must be why they shone—

Oh brother. She couldn't allow herself to get distracted, even if it were by a handsome man with a pair of fine eyes. She had too many other things to accomplish during her visit—namely, reconciling with her sister. And that meant finding a way around this ridiculous law.

Of course, being rude to her sister's friends was uncalled for. Sarah shifted the laptop to her other arm. "You didn't. I'm just trying to solve a problem for Ginny using my specific skill set, but things are not going well."

"Sad to hear that. What do you do?" Michael leaned against the wall in the dim hallway, which was lined with various photos: Ginny and Steven, Ginny and a bride with black hair and arresting blue eyes, even an old family portrait from when Sarah, Ginny, and Benjamin were teens.

If Sarah had been treated like her sister had been, the last thing she'd want hanging in her hallway was a photo of the people who had scorned her and her dreams. Was this what forgiveness looked like? And how had she managed to forgive them at all?

Sarah cleared her throat. "I'm an attorney for my father's company and work on the side for a nonprofit that provides counsel for women leaving abusive relationships. Ginny's having a legal issue of sorts with her bakery and asked me to look into it. Well, I volunteered."

Michael watched her, and his silence urged Sarah to continue.

She explained in short detail what was happening with Ginny's bakery and the parish code. "Regardless, I can't seem to find much information about the ordinance, other than that it was instituted something like a few hundred years ago. There was probably a reason for it back then, but maybe it's an old forgotten law that's no longer applicable. Anyway, someone—presumably Trengrouse or his daughter —has dug it up to keep Ginny from opening her bakery."

"Have you tried contacting the parish council?"

"Yes, but I haven't received an answer yet." Sarah

sank against the wall next to Michael. The air around them was quiet, still. "There's a parish council meeting in a week and a half, but I'd love to give Gin some peace of mind in the meantime. If I can't, though, I'll see if we can add an item to the meeting agenda."

"Maybe you just need to talk to Rebecca about it. I've known her my whole life. We grew up in the same grade in school. She's a bit of a tough nut to crack but not unreasonable. Maybe all of this can be solved with a simple friendly conversation."

"Well, it wasn't *friendly* of her to just leave that note on my sister's door, was it?" Sarah ignored Michael's amused smirk and inhaled. "But you're right. Going directly to the source never hurts." She glanced at her watch. Late afternoon. "Rebecca is probably still at the bakery, unless it closes early in the afternoon. Do you know?"

Quick as a flash, he reached out and pinched Sarah's elbow. "Hold on there, Iron Lady. Maybe you want to take some time to think of how to approach her in a less . . ."

"Intense way?"

"Exactly." Michael pushed himself off the wall. "And I know just the thing to distract you. Would you like to come with me to the bakery and take that tour?"

Sarah considered him for a moment. Perhaps a

change of scenery would be good for her. "All right. Give me just a minute and we can go."

THEY STEPPED INSIDE THE BAKERY, and Sarah observed the small area where booths and tables lined the walls and filled in the open space, providing seating for thirty or so patrons. The neutral white paint and blank walls gave the room an impersonal feel, though the fun gray-and-white diamond pattern that traversed the entire front of the bakery granted it some charm.

A wraparound display case met the polished marble counter where the cash register sat, and behind it, a currently empty gray wooden built-in boasted plenty of rows and nooks for decor, mugs, and the like. White subway tiles lined the wall surrounding the built-in. There should have been a menu somewhere, but Sarah couldn't locate one. Maybe Ginny was still finalizing it.

As she took in the surroundings, Sarah cringed at the obvious ways her sister was falling behind schedule. Then again, Ginny had never been as fastidious as Sarah. At least this meant there were numerous ways Sarah might be able to help Gin, especially since she wasn't making much progress with the legal assistance.

"I think she's back that way." Michael's words interrupted Sarah's thoughts.

They headed through a swinging door to the back of the bakery and found Ginny and Steven staring at each other like adorable, lovesick fools as Ginny shoved a beignet into Steven's mouth. He chewed, his eyes rolling back playfully in his head. "Brilliant. Absolutely brilliant."

"You think so?" Ginny's squeal evidenced her delight.

"You did it. Somehow, you made a better beignet than you have ever done."

"I want to try one." Michael's booming voice made Steven and Ginny turn.

A blush crossed Ginny's cheeks. She dusted powdered sugar off her hands and pulled a platter from the countertop, holding the golden drops of heaven under Michael's nose. "Have at it."

He took one from the platter and popped it into his mouth. "You're right, mate. It's perfection."

"Sarah? You want one?" Ginny's eyes turned shy. Maybe there was something in her that sought her big sister's approval after all.

Full from all the pastries yesterday, a beignet was absolutely the last thing she wanted, but Sarah stepped forward and snagged one anyway. "You're going to make me fat, little sis."

"I honestly doubt that." Michael's words floated

toward her in a soft cadence, but Sarah heard them nonetheless.

Something inside her swelled at the thought. Did he find her attractive?

Why does it matter? You're kind of still dating Warren.

The thought rankled. She hadn't even had time to do much more than text Warren about her last-minute trip, though she had remembered to ask him to her parents' Christmas Eve party. Of course he'd said yes. Did that count as dating?

Sarah finished off the beignet, which melted in her mouth in seconds, and washed away the crumbs in the sink. She turned her attention back to Ginny. "Michael is here to take photos for you."

"Yes, sorry. I forgot to let you know we'd be here instead."

"No worries." Michael placed his camera bag on the white quartz countertop that gleamed under the recessed kitchen lighting. Shrugging out of his jacket, he began to pull out camera parts and assemble them.

"I've put everything I'd like you to photograph over there." Ginny indicated the far counter under a window, where natural light from the slightly cloudy day drifted in. "Arrange them however you think they look best. Do you need me to stay and help?"

"Whatever you'd like. I'm happy to free up your

time if you need to do other things, but if you want to stay and make sure you're happy with the result, that's okay too." Michael placed an expensive-looking lens onto the camera. Sarah couldn't take her eyes off the way his fingers moved. Quick but sure.

He caught her staring, and she swiveled so hard to the right that her knee banged against a lower cabinet. She clenched her teeth to keep from crying out.

"Great. Steven was going to go over the website with me, and then Sophia and I were going to review details for opening day."

Sarah had yet to meet Sophia, Ginny's best friend and soon-to-be business partner. They had commissioned a door between the bookstore and bakery so patrons could easily flow from one to the other. She needed to poke her head inside Rosebud Books soon. How had she done so little with her time here so far?

But before she could open her mouth to ask if she could accompany Ginny, Michael spoke up again. "Sarah, would you like to stay and help me with the shoot?"

"Me?" Sarah dashed him a confused look. What did she know about photography?

But her gut felt sucker-punched at the pure . . . something . . . in his eyes. What was it? Admiration? But why? There wasn't much to admire in the way

Sarah had acted toward him so far. Not cold exactly, but definitely not warm.

And yet, everything about this man screamed at Sarah to trust him. Maybe it was in the way he seemed to really see her—and to be quiet enough to really listen.

But that was unnerving because it meant she'd have to speak. To share her heart. And in her experience, doing that only warranted cold glares and the silent treatment. Melissa was the only person who really knew Sarah anymore. For some reason, her friend hadn't gone running the other direction. Melissa was brave like that.

Still, Michael wasn't asking for Sarah to reveal her deepest, darkest secrets. He just wanted her to stay and help him out. She could do that. It was better than beating her head against the laptop looking for answers. "Sure."

"Great."

Ginny and Steven scampered out—but not before her sister shot Sarah a questioning arch of her brow.

Taking a white ceramic plate, Michael stacked four brownies in the foreground, twisting each one slightly to make a more artful arrangement. Next, he positioned the other brownies around the pile in a way that seemed random to Sarah, but—judging by his furrowed brow—made sense to him. There was something mesmerizing about watching him work.

The end result of his efforts made her crave . . . the brownies.

Just the brownies.

Liar.

Michael stared at the plate for a moment. Then, he picked up a brownie and turned to her. "Would you mind taking a bite out of this one?"

Sarah jerked a step back, blinking hard. "What?"

He walked the few feet toward her then held the brownie up to her mouth. "The picture. I'm going for a certain effect." He winked.

"Um, sure." She leaned in to take a bite, and he pulled it away. Sarah should have been annoyed. Instead, a smile flitted across her lips. "Really? The last time someone did that to me, I believe I was in seventh grade."

"You were that young the last time someone flirted with you?" He shook his head. "What a pity."

The words struck a match to something buried deep inside of her, but she pushed the feeling of light away, cocked a hip, and threw on the sassiest tone she could muster. "If this is you flirting, then I suppose I should prepare for you to pull my pigtails next?"

"I would if you had pigtails and not that endearing little bun." Michael angled toward her, and the spicy bergamot scent of him enveloped her. How had he managed to get so close? They stood toe-to-toe, and as she glanced up, the teasing look in his eyes turned to something more serious.

Ignoring it, she placed her hand against his solid chest and pushed back. "Fine." Leaning in, she took a small bite of brownie. After savoring the chocolate, she swallowed, licking her teeth for any remaining bits. "Satisfied?"

"Perfectly." He set the dessert on top of the stack on the plate, and the air around her that had been so warmed by his presence cooled as he moved on to his next task.

This was getting ridiculous. Of course, he was attractive, and many women would take the opportunity to flirt and have a good time with him. But Sarah had never been one of those women. She'd dated, yes, but it had mostly been for show. Warren Kensington was the first guy in a good long while who had seemed interested in more than dating "George Bentley's daughter," but had *that* even been real?

When had finding a guy who saw past her family's money to who Sarah was ever happened? Never, that's when.

The thought that it could happen here was just laughable. Michael was a handsome guy who, yes, made her feel a bit unsteady. But in Sarah's experience, flirting and forever didn't go hand in hand. She'd be better off with someone like Warren. At least she'd know what to expect with that kind of guy, even if they quite possibly lacked the spark she'd always dreamed of for her love life. But sparks had grown from mutual respect before, and if she could learn to trust Warren's intentions, then perhaps . . .

Settling in, Sarah watched Michael work for a full hour, helping him arrange things, even lending her hand for a few shots. Finally, he straightened. "I have an idea, if you're amenable."

"Need me to take a bite out of something else, do you?" Somehow, Sarah's laugh came easier now after time spent in his presence. "You people are seriously trying to blow me up like a blimp." Eyeing a cake batter cookie on the top of a pile Michael had just finished photographing, she reached around him— her hand skimming his side—snagged it, and popped a bite into her mouth.

At his raised eyebrow, she swallowed and shrugged. "What? You were finished, weren't you?"

He chuckled. "I was. And I do like watching you taste Ginny's sweets. They seem to have a way of breaking down your defenses."

"What's that supposed to mean?"

"Don't take offense. You just get this relaxed look on your face, and it's clear you're enjoying yourself." He paused, then in slow motion lifted his hand to her lips.

Sarah stilled. What . . .

But his thumb merely brushed the corner of her

mouth and was gone. "Sorry. You had a crumb on your face."

For a moment, neither of them moved. The rush of blood in her ears blocked everything out around Sarah until all she could focus on was the man in front of her.

Michael coughed. "Uh, I had a thought about your legal problem. That's what I was going to say."

"Oh?" She blinked her focus back into view.

"If you'd like, I can go with you to chat with Rebecca. Perhaps a friendly face will make things less awkward and . . . less intense."

Less intense. She could use some of that. "That would be great. Thank you."

"So . . . tomorrow, then?"

"Okay. Tomorrow."

CHAPTER 5

The word "charming" perfectly described Trengrouse Bakery, with its striped awning and window display case full of artisan bread, scones, croissants, and Victoria sponge cakes.

However, the same could not be said of its owner's daughter.

As Sarah stepped into the crowded bakery on Friday morning, with Michael beside her, her gaze narrowed on a woman with dishwater blond hair who was bustling around behind the counter. Everything about her was small, from her petite stature to her nose, ears, and mouth. But the most striking thing about her was the scowl she wore as she pulled a wrapped pastry away from an elderly man with a cane who was standing at the front of the line.

"Roderick, you are one pound short again. This is not a charity!" Her voice carried across the space, which wasn't difficult since the small room covered maybe a few hundred square feet for standing, at best, with a few tables along the wall.

One little boy pressed his face against the glass case of sweets connected to the counter, and customers waited in line chatting among themselves. Most seemed to ignore Rebecca's outburst.

"But Rebecca, your da' always let me put it on me tab."

A pinched expression flashed across Rebecca's features. "As you can see, it's just me. And I require payment now." The bagged pastry in question was in both their grips, the man's wrinkled and spotted fingers beginning to loosen.

"Oh, for goodness's sake. This is not how people should treat their customers." Without waiting for Michael to follow, Sarah dug in her purse and pulled out her wallet. Circumventing the line, she found herself face-to-face with the woman who wanted to run Ginny out of business before she'd even begun. "Here." Whipping out a credit card, she gave it to Rebecca. "It's on me."

"Thank ye, lassie. Tis verra kind." Roderick took the pastry and hobbled away.

Rebecca glared at Sarah but ran her credit card through the register all the same. "He'll never learn if people keep paying for him." Pulling the printed receipt from the machine, she shoved a pen into Sarah's hand. "Sign here, please."

Was this woman always this pleasant?

"Hullo, Rebecca." Michael joined Sarah at the counter as she signed the receipt and handed it back to the unfriendly blond. "How's business?"

"Michael." Rebecca jabbed the receipt onto a spike where a stack of others rested beneath it on the counter. "It's fine, as you can see. People still know where to go in this town to get the best breakfast and desserts around."

"Great. We—this is Sarah Bentley, by the way."

Rebecca narrowed her eyes but nodded.

"We wanted to talk with you about the letter you sent to Sarah's sister, Ginny Rose."

"I'm a little busy if you hadn't noticed."

"We won't take much of your time. Can you call Louise out here to give a hand at the counter while we chat?"

Considering him a moment, Rebecca finally turned to a window that showed through to the kitchen. "Hey, Louise! Get out here, will you?"

Sarah couldn't hold back her grimace. How was she ever going to talk some sense into this woman? At least the attorneys she dealt with on a daily basis back home pretended to have some manners.

Once a rotund middle-aged woman ambled out from behind the door, Rebecca indicated a table in the corner that a young couple had just vacated. She and Michael followed Rebecca to the table then followed her direction to sit.

"Well? You have three minutes."

Sarah took in a breath of air scented with warm blueberries, cinnamon, and coffee. Her body relaxed at the delicious smells that contrasted with the sour expression this woman wore. "About the letter you sent to Ginny. I just have to ask—"

"Why I'd do such a thing?" Sarcasm dripped from her tone.

"Yes, actually. It seemed—" *Immature. Rude. Overdone.* "A bit hasty."

"Hasty? That little tart thinks she can run my dad out of a business he built from the ground up, and *I'm* the hasty one?"

Tart? "Excuse me?" Sarah lifted a finger, a sudden desire to jab it in Rebecca's face racing through her veins, but Michael snagged her hand and pulled it beneath the table before she could. The movement—and subsequent stroking of his thumb against the top of her knuckles—took Sarah so off guard that her next words flew completely out of mind.

Michael beamed at Rebecca. "How long have you been back now? A few months? What were you doing before this?"

"Three and a half months, actually. And why the sudden interest? You haven't talked to me since high school." Folding her arms across her chest, Rebecca leaned back in her chair.

High school? Michael had made it sound like Rebecca was at least a friend.

The air crackled with intensity. This was getting them nowhere. Sarah would just have to deal with Rebecca the same way she dealt with any threat to her family's business—as a ruthless attorney. Not who she liked to be, but who she had to be.

Sarah leaned forward, lowering her voice. "Look, Rebecca, you don't know me, and I don't know you. But here's the thing I do know: My sister talked with your father, and he was OK with retiring. So why do you suddenly seem to have a score to settle?"

"My father is sick and not in his right mind at the moment." Talking between clenched teeth, Rebecca growled her words. "So forgive me if I don't much believe that he's willing to just give up the bakery he loved more than anything. And I do mean anything."

Sympathy shot through Sarah. How well she understood one's father loving work and money more than his own family. But Rebecca couldn't be allowed to play dirty just because she had daddy issues.

Michael squeezed her hand. Or was she squeezing his? Did he sense what she was feeling? But how could he possibly?

Time for this to be done and over with. Sarah pushed herself abruptly away from the table, her chair squawking loudly in the enclosed space that had grown warmer and warmer the longer she sat— and not only from the large convection ovens holding numerous trays of cookies, croissants, muffins, pies, and other delectable baked goods she'd spied just behind the door to the kitchen.

Towering over Rebecca, Sarah leaned forward. "You know that law you dug up won't hold water in court. I'm an attorney and I'll make sure of it."

A smirk crossed Rebecca's lips as she stood. Though she barely came to Sarah's shoulders, the woman held her ground, fists clenched at her sides. "From what I hear of her, Ginny Rose won't open that bakery if there's the slightest chance she'll upset people. And even if the law is declared illegitimate, by the time that's declared, her loan will come due, and she won't have the funds to pay without a working business, now will she?" Rebecca turned on her heel and stomped back to the counter, head held high.

Sarah stared after her. The woman was infuriating but she was also right. If the case got tied up in court, Ginny might not be able to open a bakery for months or even years past her original planned date. And by then . . .

Perhaps Sarah could wrangle the money for the loan. She didn't yet have access to her trust fund, not until she "married appropriately," but—

"We should probably go." Michael's whispered words breathed warmth against Sarah's ear, sending a shiver up her spine.

Her attention turned from Rebecca to the other patrons openly watching and discussing the American who'd just been verbally smacked down by one of their own. However horrid a person, Rebecca was the insider here and Sarah the outsider.

Sarah nodded and allowed Michael to lead her from the bakery.

The wind whipped at the bottom of her jacket as they exited. Morning light streamed through the clouds. Down the hill, the water in the harbor bubbled and rocked the boats in a jaunty dance. A mom with her three children examined fruit in the boxes out front of the grocer's storefront, and the scent of cooked fish steamed from the vents of a local eatery.

Port Willis was indeed a lovely little community, a few citizens notwithstanding. No wonder Ginny wanted to make a life here. But if Sarah couldn't find a way to roust Rebecca Trengrouse, then her sister would have to sacrifice her dream.

"I can't believe that went so poorly." Sarah buried her face in her hands.

"Rebecca has definitely grown tougher over the years."

She peeked at him, studying the way he tugged at a few curls at the nape of his neck that had slipped from underneath his beanie. "I'm used to tough. You should see the people I've had to go up against in court."

Michael started walking down toward the bay,

and Sarah matched his steps. "And you like that? Being an attorney?"

Folding her arms across her chest, Sarah sighed, her eyes focused on the horizon. Clouds dotted the crystal-blue sky, fluffy like an abundance of cotton balls falling all over themselves. "No. I mean, I hate the constant fighting. But it's sometimes rewarding."

"In what way? Financially?"

"No."

He stopped midstride at her sharp retort, and a flush warmed her cheeks.

"Sorry, that came out . . . Well, here's the thing, OK? I don't know if Ginny told you this, but our family is quite wealthy. And I hate it. I've always hated it, but never more than now. Because . . ." Oh, there she went, dangerously close to the edge. Wanting to step over, just to see what it felt like to reveal a piece of herself to someone other than Melissa.

But also terrified of what might happen, of what might crumble beneath her feet if she did.

They had reached the water. Seeming to sense Sarah's need for some quiet, Michael pointed to a path off to one side that led up to a grassy bluff overlooking the harbor. They hiked upward for a few minutes then stopped at the crest. From here she could see what seemed like the entire village, and even though there was a sharp drop-off less than ten feet away, she somehow also felt safe, secured away from all the world.

Sarah drew in a deep breath and sat, her knees pulled into her chest. Michael lowered himself beside her, their shoulders brushing, together watching a boat glide past the harbor's quay into the open sea, free from its constraints. With him beside her and the sun burning overhead, the slight chill in the air didn't affect her quite so much.

"Thank you for trying to help me with Rebecca."

"My pleasure." He plucked a strand of the grass that surrounded them, folding it over and over in his fingers. "You know, it's funny. Though I would never say you're rude like her and would most definitely say you're much more charming, I have to admit that the two of you are rather alike, in that you're just women trying to protect their loved ones."

"Are you chastising me?" Despite the light accusation in her tone, she genuinely wanted to know. In fact, her stomach twisted at the thought he might say yes.

Why did this man's good opinion mean so much to her?

Michael tossed the grass away and scooted back so he faced her, pinning Sarah with a look that turned her bones into liquid. "No. I just always find it helpful to look at things from another's perspective."

"Oh." Sarah's hold loosened and she allowed her

legs to straighten in front of her. "Yes, I can see the value in that."

"What I want to know most is why you feel such a need to protect Ginny."

"She's my sister."

"Yes, and I'd feel the same way about my sister Mary. But you're carrying it like a burden. It's not your problem to solve."

"But it is. I'm the one with a law degree." Sarah watched as the boat from earlier disappeared over the crest of the horizon.

"True. But Ginny seems content to trust God to work it all out."

So Michael believed too. That made sense, really, he with his constant smile. Sarah remembered that fleeting happiness, how it had felt to relish trusting in someone other than herself to make things happen.

But she'd seen too much of the world since then. People would chew you up and spit you out if you let them.

"I don't know about God, but I let her down once. I'm not going to do it again."

CHAPTER 6

If Sarah couldn't solve Ginny's legal problems, she'd do her best with the other stuff.

"Which one do you like more?" Sarah held up the two sample paint cards while her sister sorted through all the knickknacks spread across the white countertop in the front of the bakery. They'd spent all day yesterday shopping in Port Willis and surrounding towns in an attempt to find the perfect decor to complete the modern look Ginny was going for at Once Upon a Time.

Ginny glanced up and waved her hand. "Whatever you think."

Studying the canary yellow card next to the light teal, Sarah shook her head. "This is your bakery. You're going to have to live with the accent wall color every day, not me."

Blowing some errant wisps of bangs from her eyes, Ginny pulled out her ponytail holder and smoothed her hands over her long locks. "Yeah, but I really don't know. Like, I absolutely love the yellow. It feels bright and most like me. But is it too much for an entire wall? And what if I choose the wrong color and then hate it and have to stare at it forever and ever because it would be such a pain to repaint it?" She looped the elastic band around her hair.

Sarah couldn't help it. Laughter burst forth. "Okay, Miss Dramatic." Closing her eyes, she tried to imagine both colors up on the long wall opposite the door.

As she stood there picturing it, the utter quiet struck her. It was Sunday, and according to Ginny, that's when Port Willis just about shut down, especially in the wintertime. Everyone spent the day with their families—some even attended church—then tucked themselves away, resting before things began again on Monday.

In Boston, noise always surrounded the city. Horns honking. People shouting. Sirens blaring. Music bopping. Sarah usually enjoyed the constant movement—maybe because it kept her from thinking too hard about things and the way she wished they were. But wishing didn't make things happen. Doing did.

"You OK, sis?"

Ginny's question brought Sarah back to reality.

She opened her eyes. "Just trying to think about what color I'd choose if I were you." Sarah set the cards on the counter, along with the assortment of candles, tea canisters, white and yellow mugs, and the rest of the items they'd bought yesterday. Their biggest and best score had been a set of three large metal pendant light fixtures made from vintage bakery whisks that they'd purchased from an antique store in town. Steven planned to stop by later today to hang them above the front counter.

They were modern and different from Sarah's taste, which made it more difficult for her to help Ginny with her vision. "Maybe you should forego an accent wall and just use accented decor instead. You can always change that out without too much hassle."

"Oh, that's a great idea." Ginny ran her fingers over a few other knickknacks they'd picked up. "I think I like the yellow, then."

"Good choice." Sarah held up a mini chalkboard. "This feels more shabby-chic."

Ginny touched a finger to her chin, pondered the sign, and agreed. "I thought I may go that direction at first. You know, because of calling it Once Upon a Time."

Sarah snagged a few yellow mugs and studied the built-in behind the counter before placing them on one in the middle. "Why did you choose that name?"

"Partly because we're adjoining the bookstore with it. Fairy tales and all that."

"That makes sense." Sarah grabbed a knife and sliced the tape from a sealed box. Nestled inside was a yellow- and white-spotted tea kettle and matching strainer—all for display since Gin would be using her fancy other tools to make hot tea. "So why not go shabby chic, then?"

"Don't you remember the room I had growing up?"

"Yes. It was gorgeous and I was jealous. I would have loved a pink room with a lacy white comforter." The Styrofoam surrounding the tea kettle squeaked as Sarah pulled the delicate item free. "Instead I got a nautical-themed room with clean, angular lines." She held the kettle out to Ginny, who took it and arranged it on one of the shelves.

"Mother never really cared what we wanted, did she?"

"Still doesn't. Neither does Father." Sarah shoved the empty box shut and moved it to the ground. At her sister's silence, she turned.

Ginny continued to unpack colorful plates and cups and place them onto the shelves. What was she thinking? In the five days since Sarah had arrived, they'd had pleasant conversation. Sure, it was surface level, but that suited Sarah just fine. Because what was she going to say? She couldn't change the past. All she could do was use her time here to help Ginny now.

She still couldn't believe her sister hadn't been more upset yesterday when Sarah had finally gathered the courage to tell her she couldn't figure out her legal problem. But maybe that was because she'd grown so used to her family disappointing her that it didn't surprise her anymore. Or maybe Ginny had more faith in Sarah than Sarah did in herself. After all, they still had a shot at addressing the law at the parish council meeting. But that wasn't for eight more days. At least Sarah had been able to contact the council and add a motion to the meeting's agenda.

Finally, Ginny turned to Sarah and leaned against the built-in case. "You know why else I chose the name Once Upon a Time Bakery?"

"Why?"

"Because I used to believe in fairy tales. Before Garrett destroyed that belief. And now . . . well, I believe again but in a different way."

"How is it now?" Sarah joined her sister behind the counter, leaning a hip against the counter.

Ginny smiled. "Before, I thought a heroine had to go out and make her own destiny. Like, if I didn't save the business and get my husband back, then I was a failure. But now, I know that so much of a fairy tale ending is about trusting God to fight for me."

Huh. "So, you just wait around for God to do things for you?" When Sarah had first found her faith, she'd been so young, but she'd still read through the Bible at a voracious pace—the Bible she'd found tucked away on a dusty shelf in their Nantucket estate's massive library.

One day, she'd returned to her room to find the Bible missing and a biography about "strong women" in its place. A note in her father's handwriting said, "If you're looking for inspiration, find it here."

Sarah hadn't thought about that moment in a long time. About the way her teenage heart had plummeted with the loss of that precious book. About how, to avoid a confrontation, she'd read the biography cover to cover and had never gone searching for the Bible again.

But now, she couldn't help wondering—what if she had? Might things be different?

Might *she* be different?

Ginny fiddled with a snagged thread at the end of her sleeve. "No, not at all. We still move forward and follow our dreams—our dreams, not the ones people have for us—but we don't take things on our own shoulders. We know that God works all things together for good and that even when we feel like we've lost control, he hasn't. So even if this bakery fails, *I* won't be a failure." Ginny's lips twisted. "I am probably not explaining that very well. I'm still pretty new to this having-faith-thing. We definitely weren't raised that way, were we?"

"No, we weren't." Her sister had never known about Sarah's clandestine trips to her friend's youth group. How would she, when Sarah hadn't told a soul . . . until she'd heard a sermon about sharing faith with those you love, and something had stirred in her spirit. She'd gathered her courage one night to finally tell her parents about her new belief.

Instead of agreeing to try out church as a family, her parents had grounded her for "sneaking around" and had implemented a schedule that was so full she no longer had time to attend youth group.

Sarah shifted. How had Ginny come to her newfound beliefs? "Gin—"

"Hello!" The door between the bookstore and bakery opened, and Sophia Rose stuck her head inside. "Can we come in?"

Ginny straightened and squeezed Sarah's arm. "To be continued." Then she turned to Sophia, whom Sarah had met last night at dinner. "Come on in, you guys."

Sophia Rose, the gorgeous raven-haired beauty from the bridal photo on Ginny's wall, waltzed in with her shoulders high and a smile highlighting her cheekbones. Behind her came her husband, a tall and lean man with curly blond hair and thick glasses. William fit the literature professor persona better than anyone Sarah had ever seen, with his sweater vest and collared shirt rolled to reveal his forearms. Sophia's adorable slightly rounded belly whispered of the couple's upcoming blessing, due in April, if Sarah remembered correctly.

William carried what appeared to be a casserole dish wrapped in a towel. "Where do you want this, Gin?"

"This way." After giving Sophia a quick hug, Ginny led them into the kitchen, propping open the door so everyone could scoot inside.

William deposited the dish onto the counter. "Be right back." He headed through the swinging door once more, leaving the three women alone.

"What's all this?" Ginny peeked under the foil covering the casserole dish. Sarah caught a whiff of onion and roasted meat. "You didn't . . ."

Sophia laughed and placed her hand on her stomach in the way pregnant women did without seeming to realize it. "Of course I didn't make that. Becoming a wife hasn't changed my culinary skills." She turned to Sarah. "What your sister is so delicately pointing out is that, of my many talents, cooking and baking belong to her and her alone."

A former social worker and victim of domestic violence, Sophia now volunteered at a crisis center for other victims when she wasn't running the bookstore. When they'd learned of their shared passion for helping victims, she and Sarah had fallen into easy conversation last night.

"I'm with you there." As Sarah's stomach perked up, she nudged Ginny away so she could glance at the food. "Are these Cornish pasties?" The shortcrust pastry was golden brown with a flaky texture and braided cooked dough along one edge where it had sealed in the filling.

"It is indeed. Mrs. Lincoln dropped them by for all of us."

"Oh, that was so sweet and considerate." Ginny replaced the foil on the dish and moved to pull some plates from her cabinet.

"She's the one who owns the antique shop, right?" Not even one week here and Sarah had already met half the town. "Wasn't her brother there too?"

"Yes, he and his wife moved back to town recently to help her out. She's got gout, poor thing, but she still finds time to serve everyone else in town." Sophia tucked a strand of hair behind her ear and joined Ginny in getting out what they needed for the meal.

"Speaking of the Lincolns"—Ginny ducked behind the massive refrigerator door and emerged with some water bottles and soda—"when are Oliver and Joy coming into town?"

Sarah scurried over and took a few from her arms. "Who are they?"

"Oh, sorry. Joy is Sophia's best friend from America. She came here last Christmas for Sophia's wedding and fell in love with a Brit."

Glancing between Sophia and Ginny, Sarah quirked an eyebrow. "I'm sensing a theme."

The women burst out laughing.

Sophia winked at her. "Be careful or it'll happen to you too."

Michael's face flashed in her mind. Not only that but the way he'd sat with her on Friday, enjoying the quiet and the view. She'd thought about that way too often during the last few days.

But fall in love? No way. She didn't even have the luxury of a flirtation, not with Warren waiting in the wings and the weight of her father's expectations on her shoulders.

A water bottle tumbled from Sarah's hands and rolled across the floor. She set the rest of the drinks on the counter and picked the chilly plastic container off the ground.

Would it be too much to hope that Ginny and Sophia would just think she was clumsy?

Clearing her throat, Sarah placed her hands on her hips. "Sorry, I distracted you from Ginny's original question."

After a confused look passed across Sophia's face, she smiled. "Oh yeah. Pregnancy brain." She stuck out her tongue just slightly and turned to Ginny. "Joy and Oliver are planning to come to your opening and stay through New Year's."

"They don't live here?" Sarah asked.

"No, she's from Florida and her parents are there," Sophia said. "She didn't want to leave them because her mom has Alzheimer's. So they did the long-distance thing for a while then got married about six months ago. Oliver moved to Florida and travels back to London about every other month for work."

"That's sweet how they worked it out."

William returned with a side of peas and gravy and placed it onto the counter next to the pasties. He snagged a plate then handed it to Sophia, stealing a quick kiss before he released it.

With all the horrible relationships Sarah constantly saw back home—men who treated their women like garbage or even people like her parents who never showed affection and treated each other as indifferent acquaintances—she could definitely appreciate the change in scenery.

And as she dished up her Cornish lunch and joked and laughed with her sister and her friends, the natural warmth of the kitchen seemed to reach out and wrap Sarah in its arms, beckoning her to lean into this place.

If she weren't careful, Port Willis and its people were going to be hard to leave come December 23.

CHAPTER 7

This was never going to work.

Sarah paced the length of Ginny's hallway, turned on her heel, then paced back the way she'd come. Studying the stack of papers in her left hand, she sipped from a coffee mug using her right. The words on the page blurred together, which was unsurprising considering how late she'd been up the night before writing her notes.

Hair hung in her eyes and she blinked in rapid motion. "Just keep going, Sarah. Just keep moving, moving, moving."

Great, now she was talking to herself. But someone had to motivate her. Since Sarah had spent last Sunday decorating, her sister was one week closer to the opening date of her bakery but no closer to actually being able to open it. Yes, Sarah had helped apply some paint, hang the menu, arrange the decor, and select some more last-minute trinkets to enhance the character of the space, but Ginny's legal problems were not just going to go away.

And unless Sarah wowed the parish council at tomorrow night's meeting, Ginny could kiss her dreams of owning a bakery goodbye.

As much as she said she trusted God to fight for her, Ginny had to be worried. Sarah saw the more prominent crease in her brow, the way her lips drew taut when she didn't think anyone was looking. Yet, still she acted like she believed in God's ability to handle it.

If only Sarah were as confident.

"Argh." She threw the papers against the wall. Instead of a satisfying thud, the papers fluttered to the ground as slow as they pleased.

"Wow."

Sarah glanced up at the sudden intrusion, the movement sending her coffee sloshing over the rim of the mug and all over her white sweater.

"Oh man." Michael strode forward from the doorway, snatching a towel from the kitchen counter as he came closer to Sarah. He held it out as if a peace offering.

"Don't you ever knock?" Tears welled in her eyes as she jerked the rag from his hands and ran it along the front of the cashmere. But what was the point? It was clearly ruined by her clumsiness. She dropped the towel onto the floor and sighed. "I'm sorry. That was rude."

"No, I barged in here again without thinking about how it might interrupt your work." Michael watched her for a moment, and she took the time to study him too. It had been days since she'd seen him, though they'd texted a bit here and there. He'd been working and so had she, and Sarah had declined Ginny's invitation to attend church that Sunday morning, where she would have seen him.

There was no sense in denying it. She'd missed him—his infectious laugh, that eternal optimism he seemed to possess.

She could tell him, but what would that do?

"I'm not getting anywhere with it anyway."

Michael scooped up the fallen papers and handed them to Sarah. "Is this work-work, or help-Ginny-save-the-bakery work?"

The paper crunched in Sarah's fist. "The latter. I haven't done any actual work since leaving Boston. It's been strange." Yes, she'd checked in with Melissa almost daily regarding New Dawn work and called Elise several times since their first meeting two weeks ago, but that didn't feel like work. She'd kept busy trying to help her sister, but something deep inside craved working toward something with purpose.

Not that a bakery didn't have purpose. She just

didn't feel like she was doing much to truly help Ginny. Anyone could paint and decorate.

It all came back to tomorrow night's meeting. And the papers in her hand were proof that she didn't have any leverage, no matter what angle she tried.

Her jaw ached and head pounded. The answers should have been there, but if they were, Sarah couldn't find them.

"Hey, so I know I can't help much with it, but I do know when someone needs a break. And you are definitely there." Michael eased the papers from Sarah's hands and laid them on the kitchen counter. "Go get changed. I've got just the thing."

"No, I need to figure this out. It won't get done if I do something else."

"Actually, I've found when I'm having a creative block, doing something else is the exact thing I need." Michael placed his hands on her shoulders, his lightly twitching thumbs shooting a spark through her insides.

Sarah's breathing hitched at his nearness. "What did you have in mind?"

A grin spread across his face. "You'll just have to trust me."

That was the trouble. She did. But why? She'd only known the guy a few weeks.

She held up her forefinger. "I'll give you one hour."

"It's going to take longer than that."

She scolded her stomach as it flipped at the thought of spending extended time with him. "I'd better change then."

"We'll be walking a lot, so just maybe don't wear heels, yeah?" Michael chuckled.

"Ha ha." Sarah shoved him playfully then ducked and squealed as he tried to snatch her waist. A minute later, she found herself in Ginny's guest room, laughing and shaking her head as she threw off the soiled sweater. Reaching for her emerald green belted wrap blouse—a favorite that she'd been told made her eyes pop—her hand switched directions at the last second and landed on a long-sleeved T-shirt. She tossed it on with a pair of faded jeans and threw back her hair into a messy bun.

With her tired red eyes and casual clothing, at least no one could accuse her of trying to impress Michael.

Because she definitely wasn't. Nope.

She joined him in the kitchen and, after slipping on her parka, they headed out. Soft gray puffs clouded the sky, and the crisp air bit into her cheeks with a winter reminder of the possibility of snow coming before she left Port Willis.

The thought of returning to Boston sat sour in her stomach.

No. She wouldn't think about that. Not today.

Instead, she'd focus on the gorgeous scenery as they drove.

And yeah, maybe even the gorgeous company.

Throughout the hour-long drive, Michael snuck glances at her and asked her a slew of small-talk questions. Sarah relaxed into her seat as they chatted, her eyes taking in the peaceful countryside. They passed several other tiny villages, though none could compete with the charm of the seaside Port Willis.

Trees surrounded and arced over the road along several stretches. And even though many of their branches hung bare, there was something wondrous about them—the way they hedged the road in, almost like they were protecting it.

Eventually they arrived at what Michael said was a two hundred-acre estate with massive gardens famous in the area. He got out and opened her door for her. She climbed from the truck, taking his offered hand, which he didn't relinquish as he led her through the front office and paid for their entrance. Tugging her along one of the many trails, Michael strolled with his camera around his neck, gazing at the trees surrounding them and naming various plant life.

She should have tugged her hand away, but the way it nestled so perfectly inside his thrummed a constant glow through her—silly, considering they both wore gloves. Her cheeks heated despite the cold air turning them pink.

Their shoes crunched the gravel underneath their feet. "And that is a cluster of snowdrops." Michael pointed to a drift of low-growing plants with sturdy-looking stalks. Each stalk played host to one small white flower that drooped downward.

Currently, the flowers were closed tightly, but Sarah imagined them as they would be in their rightful glory—their petals spread wide and arching over one another.

With a little sun and patience, these beauties would bloom. What a sight that would be.

If only I could see it. But she'd be gone by then.

"They're gorgeous."

He looked from them to her, a smile quirking the side of his lips. "Yeah, they are." He squeezed her hand, dropped it, and pulled his camera from its bag. Then he snapped a few shots of the snowdrops up close. "You ever learn anything about photography?" Michael kept taking photos, but somehow she sensed he was just as attuned to her as she was to him.

"No. I had to learn how to play the piano like any good Bentley would, but that's about where our artistic education stopped."

"Pity." He straightened and turned to look at her. "You want to learn?"

She hesitated. "I don't want to drop your camera."

He tapped the strap hanging from the back. "That's what this is for."

Bits of light had started to break through the clouds and filter down, combining with the canopy of trees to create soft spotlights all around them. Here, she felt hemmed in, safe, but not trapped—finally free from the eyes constantly watching the oldest Bentley daughter and future CEO of Bentley & Co.

Here, with Michael, she was simply Sarah.

And Sarah wanted to learn a bit about photography.

She took off her gloves then stepped closer to him. "Would you mind showing me a few things?"

"I'd love to." He slipped the camera strap around her. The camera's weight strained against her neck as if the thing was trying to escape—surprising, given the effortless way Michael had held it like it weighed nothing more than a tissue.

She took the precious tool from him, her fingers brushing his. "What do I do first? I mean, I know the basics of how these work, but how do you get a good photo?"

"It's all about lighting. If you can find the right light, you're halfway to a decent photo."

"How do you know what the right light is?" Holding the camera to her eye, she squinted through the tiny viewfinder. The world narrowed but somehow that didn't make it any smaller. Instead, it allowed her to focus. She moved the lens closer to the snowdrops, zooming in to see the tiny bladed leaves on each stalk.

"When shooting outside, the early morning or a few hours before sunset are really the best times when it comes to light. You want soft, not harsh, but not so soft that there are a lot of shadows."

"Harsh is bad, soft is good. Got it." Sarah lowered the camera and found Michael staring at her. Glancing away, she bit her lip and studied the cluster of buttons on the back of the camera. "But it looks like there are a lot of settings on this thing. I'm thinking there's more to it than you're letting on."

"Here, may I?"

"Of course." But before she could unloop the camera from her neck, he stepped up beside her and took the camera in his right hand while she kept hold of it in her left. Their shoulders pressed against each other, and his left arm slipped around her shoulders as he leaned in, making adjustments to the buttons on the camera.

Sarah could hardly breathe with his nearness as she watched his thumb fly.

"There. It's ready for you. Just aim and shoot."

She swallowed, afraid to look up at him—of what she'd see there and of what she'd reveal of the butterflies tumbling about in her chest. "But you didn't teach me anything." Not that she could have really focused on any lessons at this moment anyway.

"My first lesson is that you just need to feel it out. Find joy in the doing before getting bogged down in all the details. Just have fun."

She nearly laughed. Fun. What was that?

"I'll try." Taking the camera fully in her possession again, Sarah repositioned the viewfinder. Michael stepped back to give her space. The tension in her shoulders dropped with the distance, but so did her heart at having him farther away.

But it put her alone with the camera—just her and a world of possibility. In this moment, the only thing that mattered was *her* perspective, how she saw the world. That's what would be recorded. Nothing more, nothing less.

She framed the snowdrops and clicked the button to take a photo, a sigh whooshing from her lungs.

After snapping several more, she glanced up. Michael leaned against a tree, hands in his jacket pockets, watching her, an indiscernible look in his eyes. "May I see them?"

Sarah managed only a nod.

He reached for the camera, his eyes not leaving hers until the last possible moment. Then he studied the photos. "These are really great, Sarah."

She looked down at them, shrugged. "They're amateur."

"They're yours and *that* makes them perfect. Don't let anyone ever tell you any differently."

A tear spilled from her eyes, and she swatted it away, praying he hadn't noticed.

Goodness, this man. If she didn't get away from here right this second, she was bound to leap into his arms and make a complete fool of herself.

Her fingers tingled as she tugged her gloves back on. "I think I'll leave the photography to the professionals. But thank you, Michael." *Thank you for seeing me.*

She started down the garden path once more, shaking the fallen leaves from her shoes.

CHAPTER 8

The best thing about being an attorney was helping people. But when Sarah failed, she once again became that green first-year law student who didn't have a clue about how things really worked.

And right here, in this moment, she was desperate to avoid that feeling.

Sarah uncrossed and recrossed her legs for the thousandth time as she listened to a local parish citizen drone on about her dislike of chickens.

Really? Chickens?

"Bottom line, I'm waking up far too early because of the noise. I'd like to propose a zoning change." The forty-something placed a hand on her ample hip and harrumphed into the microphone set up in the middle of the floor. Seven council members sat up front, the chairman in the middle, and the rest of the small room was filled with townspeople from Port Willis and a few surrounding villages.

Across the aisle, Sarah spied Rebecca Trengrouse lounging in her seat, arms crossed over her chest. No one sat with her.

Trying to keep herself from rolling her eyes at Chicken Lady, Sarah gripped the folder in her lap and smoothed the top sheet of paper that contained her outline. To her right, Ginny sat with Steven, her bobbing knee the only sign she was nervous about today's outcome. On Sarah's left sat Michael, who'd insisted on coming as moral support.

She'd received no massive revelations during their day out together yesterday, but one thing was for certain—if she spent much more time in his presence like that, she was going to kiss the man, plain and simple.

And though that idea was altogether much too pleasant, she knew it could lead nowhere. Nowhere real, anyway. What was she going to do? Run off to England like Ginny had?

And what about Warren? He'd texted her several times during the last few days to let her know how excited he was to spend Christmas Eve together. Not that they'd ever said they were exclusive. But still.

A sigh escaped Sarah's lips, and Michael's hand slipped over one of her own, giving it a quick squeeze before releasing her. She looked at him and mouthed *thank you*. Leaning toward her, he whispered, "You've got this, Sarah. I believe in you." His breath warmed her ear and neck, sending shivers up her spine.

The council voted to retain the current zoning, much to Chicken Lady's loud dismay, and moved on to the next agenda item. "Next, we have Ms. Ginny Rose with a motion to discuss and dismiss Ordinance Five Two Six Eight."

Ginny and Sarah stood and walked to the microphone, which Ginny snagged and adjusted to fit her height. "Hello, esteemed council."

If this hadn't been such a serious matter, Sarah would have snickered at her sister's formality. Ginny had never been one to enjoy speaking in public, and Mother had constantly been on her about her use of "slang." Really, it was just further proof that Ginny had always been different than the rest of the Bentleys.

But while their parents saw that as a bad thing, Sarah wished she had what Ginny possessed—a surety inside herself. Ginny knew who she was, with or without the world's approval.

With or without her family's approval.

Ginny stepped back and looked expectantly at Sarah. Oops. Sarah must have missed her introduction. No matter. She squared her shoulders and took her sister's place behind the microphone. "Thank you for allowing us the time to come before you to discuss this outdated ordinance that, if allowed to remain as part of the law, will inhibit my sister from opening a bakery in Port Willis. You see . . ."

Sarah filled in the council on the ordinance, Ginny's history with Mr. Trengrouse, and his apparent wishes before his daughter took over. "Digging up this ordinance—one that I have, in fact, seen broken by no less than three local businesses—is a last-ditch attempt by the owner's daughter to keep a monopoly over the baked goods industry in town." Glancing from council member to council member, Sarah could see she'd swayed at least three of them to her side. Most of them were, after all, businesspeople. They had to understand that monopolies were bad for villages, driving up prices and lowering quality.

"Why is she afraid of a bit of honest competition? And why is she trying so hard to maintain the business her father was fully in favor of letting go?" Maybe that last part was a low blow, but Rebecca had to take it if she was going to dish it out, right? Next to her, Ginny shifted and pressed on Sarah's arm.

Had Sarah gone too far? Perhaps. She inhaled a deep breath then leaned toward the microphone. "Thank you."

The chairman covered his microphone and conferred with one of his colleagues then nodded and looked back at Sarah and Ginny. "We appreciate you bringing this to our attention. Is the aforementioned business owner or his daughter in attendance tonight?"

"I am." Rebecca stood and waltzed to the front of the room, squeezing in beside Sarah and nudging her out of the way.

Sarah's hands curled, but Ginny grabbed one of her fists and led them back to their seats.

"Miss . . ."

"Trengrouse."

"Miss Trengrouse, please enlighten the council as to why you took it upon yourself to find this law and use it in what seems to be a scare tactic."

"Sir, that is not at all what this is." Rebecca put on a slick tone that dripped with syrup. "I simply want justice to be done. This is a law, and I feel the law should be followed. Don't you? As for the other businesses that Ms. Bentley referred to, I actually have documentation that shows they agreed amicably to disregard the ordinance in question." She held up a piece of paper.

Sarah wanted to groan. Why hadn't she investigated further?

Her face must have revealed her inner angst because to her left Michael's hand encased hers. As she listened to Rebecca go on and on about how her family had established Trengrouse Bakery in 1909 and how her relationship with her family and all her fondest memories centered around kneading bread and frosting cinnamon buns and how all of that might be ruined if the council allowed an American with no regard for Cornish tradition to come in and plow through them all, the desire to weep came harder and faster.

Not just crying. No, tears wouldn't do the feelings welling up inside of her justice.

This was a soul-deep cry from her heart, one that was watching her sister's dreams die second by second—like seeing a hangman first knotting the noose, then testing it for its strength and ability to kill, then fitting it around the dream's neck . . .

"Thank you for your input, miss. You may take your seat." The chairman glanced at his fellow members. "All in favor of dismissing Ordinance Five Two Six Eight, raise your hands."

Only one member—not even one of the ones Sarah had thought she'd snagged earlier—raised their hand.

"All opposed, raise your hands." The other six members, including the chairman, lifted their hands.

A smile twitched on the chairman's lips as he located Rebecca in the crowd. "The motion to dismiss Ordinance Five Two Six Eight is denied. And with that, our meeting is adjourned."

Although the room burst to life at that moment, to Sarah, everything stopped. The increasing volume reminded her of bees buzzing around a hive. She leaned forward and buried her face in her hands.

Ginny rubbed her back. "It's okay, sis. We'll find another way."

How was her sister the one comforting Sarah? Where was she drawing her strength, her optimism, her trust from? Certainly not from the family who had raised her then spit her out.

"But now, I know that so much of a fairy tale ending is about trusting God to fight for me." Gin's words from last week flooded back to Sarah.

It must be God, then.

What would it be like to return to the faith of her youth? What must God think of Sarah, who'd basically abandoned him in favor of her parents' religion of self-sufficiency? In their world, the only way for a person to get what they wanted was to outsmart others or work with them. It was the strategy Sarah had chosen with Father: give him herself as future CEO in exchange for New Dawn's funding.

Maybe it was too late for her. But it was not too late for Ginny. Sarah wouldn't allow someone—Rebecca Trengrouse, in this instance—to shatter her sister's faith, her spirit, her dreams.

"You're right. We will."

Sarah kept her gaze averted from Michael's, though the intensity of his eyes on her powered through the air. If she looked his way, he'd surely see the trembling, the self-doubt, the guilt. Pressing her lips together, Sarah stood and anchored herself with the only resource she had available—resolve to find a way, no matter what.

A STEADY RAIN paddled the window, plinking with abandon.

Though she tried to ignore it, the sound of every drop, like fingers tapping the glass, rang above her head. She rolled over and glanced at the clock gleaming red in the darkness—3:24 a.m. Only five minutes past the last time she'd looked.

Groaning, she rolled out from beneath the comforter, the cold floor greeting her toes before she could stuff on her slippers. Might as well get up. Her thoughts wouldn't let her sleep.

She wrapped herself in a robe Ginny had lent to her and opened the door with a quiet touch, flinching when a squeak resounded through the dim hallway. Sarah snuck past Ginny's room and into the kitchen where her sister had left a light on above the stove. As she filled a kettle with water from the refrigerator, her mind continued circling back to earlier tonight—or should she say, last night?

Rebecca Trengrouse had made fools of them all, but that wasn't what bothered Sarah most. The thing she kept coming back to wasn't really about the parish council meeting at all but rather a question Michael had asked her when they'd visited the Trengrouse bakery: *"What I want to know most is why you feel such a need to protect Ginny."*

After she turned on one of the stove's burners, she lit the gas. Once the tiny blue flame fluttered into being, Sarah placed the kettle on the range, and, after removing a mug from the cabinet and placing a bag of chamomile tea inside, leaned against the counter with arms folded across her chest.

Michael hadn't even known their family's history when he asked that question. He still didn't know everything, though bits and pieces of the story had fallen into place during their long day at the garden. Yet even he could see that something wasn't right in Sarah and Ginny's relationship.

Why *did* she feel this burning need to protect Ginny—and Ginny's dreams? She hadn't done so in the past. So why now?

The kettle whistled, startling her from her thoughts. She flicked off the burner, pulled the kettle from the stovetop, and poured the liquid into her cup. The steam curled against her cheeks as it lifted and dispersed.

Taking the mug in hand, Sarah wandered into the living room and caught sight of the bare Christmas tree. Ginny still hadn't decorated it and probably wouldn't. Christmas was what . . . ten days away? Nine? The bakery opening would be here before they knew it.

If it came at all.

Fighting the urge to hurl the mug of tea against the wall, Sarah set it down onto the coffee table instead. She strode toward the boxes under the tree and pulled open the tabs of the top one. A sparkling assortment of ornaments greeted her.

After a successful search for hooks, Sarah began to take ornaments from the box. One after another, she pressed the hooks through the caps of dainty glass icicles, porcelain balls, and sparkling snowflakes. Then she hung them on the tree, ensuring that each one shone from the perfect spot, yes, but also that they all blended into one picture, working together to create something one couldn't make on its own.

Her tea grew cold as she worked.

A noise sounded behind her, so Sarah turned. There stood Ginny, mouth slightly open as she watched. After a moment, she walked to a small stereo and turned on its radio. Kenny G or some such musician spun a soft Christmas tune throughout the room as Ginny joined Sarah at the box and lifted out an ornament. They worked in tandem, not speaking, the only sound that of a silky saxophone surrounding them.

After a while, Sarah reached into the box and felt around. Only one ornament left. She tried to hand it to Ginny, but her sister just smiled. "You do the honors."

"I don't deserve to." Heat, sudden and fierce, hammered the back of Sarah's eyelids.

Ginny's face softened and she stepped closer. "Sarah, please. Don't beat yourself up over this."

A tear escaped. "I didn't protect you, Gin. I should have. I . . . I'm so sorry."

"Oh, sis." And there came Ginny's arms around her again. "The bakery is my dream and my responsibility, not yours. If it's meant to be, it'll be. God's got a plan. I may not know what that is, and I may not even like it, but . . ." She shrugged.

Sarah shook her head, tears now falling much more freely, soaking the shoulder of Ginny's long-sleeved pajamas. "I'm not talking about the bakery." Her words came out muffled, so she pulled herself back from her sister's embrace. When Sarah looked Gin in the eyes, her sister's tears mirrored hers. "I'm talking about when Mother and Father disowned you. I should have stood up for you. I should have told them how ridiculous they were being. I should have—"

"Stop. Just . . . Sarah, come on. I don't blame you. I know the hold they have over people. They had the same hold over me."

"But you were strong enough to get out."

"Not really. I just fell in love and that was stronger than my fear." Ginny gripped Sarah's upper arms. "I don't blame *you*. I never blamed you."

"You should have, though. I've been a horrible

sister." Sarah lifted the star ornament in her hand closer to examine it. Her finger traced the golden spires, following a trail of glitter across its surface.

"I was the one who left, not you." Ginny gently nudged Sarah in the ribs. "And you're here, aren't you? You've bent over backward to help me these last few weeks. You put your life—your work—on hold to be with me. And whatever happens with the bakery, I'll never forget that. Ever."

Sarah couldn't look up again. Despite Ginny's kind and forgiving words, she couldn't get past the thought that she'd failed. But again—why did she feel such responsibility for Ginny's dreams?

Unless . . . What if it weren't really Ginny's dreams she was worried about? Was she doing all of this, feeling all of this, because she knew her own dreams would never come true—and solving Ginny's problems had become a fair substitute?

Had she done all of this for herself? That's not what she'd meant to do.

Sarah's hand trembled and she feared dropping the ornament. Once again, she tried to shove it into Ginny's hands.

Her sister's fingers wrapped around Sarah's, but she refused to take the ornament. "How about we both do it?"

"OK."

Drawing strength from her sister's confidence, Sarah pushed a hook through the ornament's top loop and closed the bottom. And with each of them holding on, they positioned the ornament at the center of the tree.

Taking a deep breath, Sarah slid her arm around Ginny's waist and laid her head on her shoulder as Bing Crosby crooned about a white Christmas.

That's when Sarah noticed it—sometime during the last hour, the rain had stopped. Moonlight peeked through the frosty window and illuminated the tree.

Together, they had made something beautiful.

CHAPTER 9

*W*as she completely out of her depth here?

Sarah clasped the plastic-wrapped plate harder as she stared through the front windows of the Village Pub. It didn't appear as crowded as usual, given the late afternoon hour on a weekday, but things would probably pick up in the next hour or two. It was now or never.

What would Michael think of her traipsing in there and giving him a tray of baked goods? That wasn't something that friends did for each other, was it? Would she be declaring too much with the gesture?

It had all seemed so logical an hour ago. She wanted to thank him for last Sunday's trip to the gardens and for his supportive presence at the parish council meeting three nights ago. What better way to do that than a dessert—one that Ginny had assured her was his favorite?

No sense standing out here in the cold, especially since snow was in the forecast sometime this week. Not even the parka hugging her torso or the cap she wore on her head kept the chill out today.

Or maybe that was the nerves talking.

When Sarah pushed open the door to the restaurant, an assortment of aromas embraced her, warm and welcoming. A fire roared in a hearth nearby.

"Welcome to the Village Pub." The hostess eyed the brownies in Sarah's hands. "Will you be dining with us today?"

"No, I was hoping to . . ." Deep breath. "Is Michael Hammett here?"

"Let me fetch him for you."

"Thank you."

After a minute or two, the hostess returned with Michael in tow. He wore a black apron over his jeans and sweater. How did an apron manage to look so manly when tied around his trim waist?

When he saw Sarah, the way his face lit up did something to her insides. *Friends, friends. We're just friends.*

"Hey, Sarah."

"Sorry to interrupt you at work." She held out the platter. "I just wanted to bring you these as a thank you."

He untied the apron and eyed the hostess, who was not-so-surreptitiously listening while pretending to study something on the podium. Reaching for the plate, his hand landed on Sarah's wrist. "Take a walk with me?"

"Oh. Sure." Ginny was in another town nearby with Sophia picking out some last-minute serving ware, so Sarah didn't need to be home at any particular time tonight. "I'm all yours."

The moment the words left her lips, her cheeks burned.

Michael's grin was his only reply as he removed the apron, deposited it on a nearby coat rack, slipped on a light-brown jacket and red-and-gray scarf, and led the way outside. He took the platter from her and peeled one corner of the plastic up to peek inside. "Brownies? Did Ginny make them?"

"No, I did." At his look of surprise, she scoffed playfully. "You didn't think she's the only one in the family who can bake? Though, admittedly, she may have loaned me her recipe."

"Excellent." He kept hold of the brownies with one hand and reached for her with the other.

Nearly without thinking, she slipped her hand inside his, and they took off down a path along the harbor. Different than the one they'd taken a few weeks ago, this path wound upward and out of town. "Where are we going?"

He pointed. "The lighthouse."

During her time here she'd noticed the white structure, which overlooked Port Willis like a stately reminder of time gone by. It was only a mile outside of the village, but between readying the bakery and keeping tabs on New Dawn, she hadn't found the time to visit.

"So, what are you thanking me for?"

The brisk air kept them walking at a quick pace instead of strolling leisurely like her heart wished they could. She wanted to enjoy every moment of her hand resting in his, of being near to this man who made her feel things she hadn't felt in a long time. Or ever, really.

But it was probably just the magic of being out from under her parents' thumbs, the gorgeous setting, the time of year—all combined to create the perfect scenario for romance.

Put her and Michael in another time and place, and he certainly wouldn't have this honeyed grip on her heart. Right?

"Sarah?"

"Sorry." On the horizon, clouds gathered and progressed toward them. "You have been really sweet while I've been here—distracting me when I needed it and helping me to get out of my head. And you've helped me try to solve a few problems too. I really appreciate it. So I wanted to thank you for being . . . such a good friend." She nearly choked on the last word.

Michael didn't speak for several moments that felt like much more. What was he thinking? "Of course." His cheeriness seemed forced, but perhaps she was reading too much into it.

Refusing to look at him, she swept her attention toward the landscape and gasped. Grassy bluffs dropped off into rocky cliffs, and the ocean below disappeared and became white foam as it crashed against them. A little farther up the path stood the white lighthouse with a bright red door. It was weathered but something about the history behind it sent shivers down her spine.

Or maybe that was the cold in the air thanks to the decreasing temperature and the clouds rolling in.

"Gorgeous."

"You think *this* is gorgeous? Come on." Once again, Michael tugged her gently away into the lighthouse. They climbed the old stone steps and emerged into a room that boasted a whole wall of windows.

Letting go of Michael's hand, Sarah put her nose nearly to the glass. Below, the entire ocean spread before them, and Port Willis was but a small blip on the horizon down the shore. "I've never seen anything like this, not even from my office back home."

Michael set the plate of brownies on the ground and fished out two, handing her one. "You work in a skyrise, don't you?"

She took the fudgy treat in hand, pulled a crumbly piece off the corner, and plopped it into her mouth. Mmm. "Yes, and the view is spectacular, especially when the sun is shining. But this . . . it's beautiful even when the clouds obscure the sun, you know?" After some thoughtful chewing, she turned to face him. "And besides, the view at my office is kind of tainted, knowing that I'm staring out from a prison of sorts."

"A prison?" He moved closer, the warmth radiating from his body.

"My job. I hate it." She finished the brownie then brushed her fingertips together. "My father is grooming me to be the CEO, and I just don't want it. But what Father wants, he gets."

Michael's brow furrowed. "Why is that? Why don't you just tell him you'd rather do something else?"

She laughed and the caustic noise grated against the silence. Outside, waves pounded the glass. Sarah wanted to pound back. "I know I'll lose one way or another."

"What do you mean?"

"I mean . . ." It was pointless to drudge up the past, wasn't it? But why not? What could it hurt to say the words? If she didn't, they might shred her from the inside out. "To my father, obedience equals love. And despite how awful he and my mom are, I love them. I'm afraid if I go against what they want for my life, what happened to Ginny will happen to me. I'll lose my family."

She felt rather than saw him lean in. "Why do you think that will happen?" He closed the small gap between them, throwing his arm across her shoulders. His clothes smelled like the restaurant—roasted meats, spices, freshly baked bread.

Comfort.

Giving in to the temptation she'd fought for so long, she placed her arms around him and snuggled into his embrace. He moved his face closer, his cheek against her forehead.

"Why? Because it's happened before. When I was thirteen, a girl in my class invited me to a lock-in with her youth group. I liked the girl—she was sweet and real, you know?—but my parents said no." Clearly, her status as a scholarship student placed her beneath the Bentleys.

With her right hand, Sarah ran her finger up and down the zipper line of Michael's coat. Despite the layers of fabric between them, his heartbeat permeated to match hers.

"I was so tired of being ruled by them, so I decided to go anyway. My parents had a charity event that night, and I told the chauffeur that I was allowed to go. Halfway through the lock-in—at midnight, if you can believe it—the chauffeur showed up. Poor Alfred. He said he was sorry then led me back to the car, where my father sat in the back seat." Sarah sighed. "He didn't say a word to me that night or for the next month."

"That's horrible. You were only a kid."

"It's just how he is. Even now, twenty years later, he has me right where he wants me."

Like a fish on a hook. And no amount of wriggling did any good.

Her breathing hitched. Michael's lips feathered a kiss across her temple—a show of support.

And maybe . . . more?

Embracing his encouragement, Sarah swallowed past the lump in her throat. "Remember the nonprofit I told you about? That's the job I really love. I founded it with a close friend of mine, and together we have helped hundreds of women out of bad situations. That's the work that feeds my soul."

"Why not just tell your dad?"

"Oh, he knows." She told him about the funding situation and the deal she had to make for the funding to stay in place.

Braving a glance upward, Sarah found Michael's face mere inches away. The compassion in his eyes was a punch in her gut, his companionship too much. All of it was melting her resolve to keep him solidly in the friend zone.

Sarah rushed on. "I mean, he's so controlling that

he even thinks he can choose who I date. Just before I came here, there was this guy . . ."

Michael's eyebrows lifted.

Why had she brought up Warren? "Never mind. The point is, for the first time, I feel almost like I could leave. Like Ginny did."

"Yeah?"

Sarah nodded. "But I know if I do, not only will I lose his love, but all of those women that New Dawn helps will have no one to fight for them. Either way, I lose something I desperately want."

"I can't imagine you would stop fighting just because you came up against some bumps in the road." His gentle voice matched the softness of his hand as he raised it to stroke Sarah's cheek. "And I'm so sorry that your father uses the word *love* to try to control you. But Sarah, you have another dad who is completely the opposite."

Another dad? Oh. "I . . . I used to believe that, once upon a time."

"What happened?"

"I was weak." She glanced down but he nudged her chin up with a finger. The constancy of Michael's gaze cracked any defenses that might have still been standing in her heart.

Her lips trembled. "After they didn't let me go to the lock-in, I became angry and defiant for the first —and only—time in my life." Until a few weeks ago, anyway. "I started sneaking off to attend youth group with Rachel, and I actually became a Christian. But I let my parents talk me out of it. And then I started to embrace their way of doing things because it was easier than fighting them. But now, I wonder if . . ."

If God could ever love me again.

He tilted his head. "Come on. I want to show you something." He pulled away from her, but only so he could lead her through a door behind them, one worn around the edges.

"Are we supposed to go in here?" It was probably closed for a reason.

"It's fine. Just an area most don't know about."

The door shut, leaving the space dark except for the light coming through a tiny window. In the middle of the room, a staircase led up to another level. That was unexpected. But now that she thought about it, there was an outdoor catwalk ringing the top of the lighthouse, wasn't there?

They took the stairs into a small lantern room. Up here they were completely surrounded by 360 degrees of glass. In the very center of the room sat a cracked lens, the glass encircling it caked with smudges. Clearly the lighthouse had been out of commission for a long time. One of the outer glass panels swung out, allowing access to the catwalk. Sarah took tentative steps out onto the metal banister and gripped the railing.

Oh wow. Everything was clearer, crisper, more

vibrant and beautiful up here. She'd thought the view amazing before, but this . . .

If she hadn't stepped out, she'd never have known what she was missing.

Sarah laughed and closed her eyes, allowing the moment to sweep over her. The ocean bellowed, showcasing its sheer power yet calling to her just the same.

She was in the middle of the coming storm but somehow also cradled in an invisible hand.

"It's majestic and enthralling and . . ." She turned to Michael and snagged his hand, tears stinging her eyes. And though her heart raced within her at the contact, right now she wasn't thinking about romance—even though she was more drawn to him than she'd ever been before.

Right now, she was thinking about another kind of love entirely. One that, she saw with new eyes, had been pursuing her throughout her entire life.

As if understanding her thoughts, Michael leaned in, pressing his forehead to hers. "Sarah, real love isn't selfish." Despite the wind and the waves, she heard him down to her toes. "Love doesn't force itself on others, isn't always 'me first,' doesn't fly off the handle, doesn't keep score of others' sins, doesn't revel when others grovel, takes pleasure in the flowering of truth, puts up with anything, trusts God always, always looks for the best, never looks back, but keeps going to the end.'"

Michael was speaking but they were words she'd read a long time ago in a book written by a father who loved her. The truth of them, like the wind, spun all around her, inviting her to dance.

So, she finally did.

CHAPTER 10

She'd made a decision—one she prayed she wouldn't come to regret.

Leaning on the pillows propped against the head-board behind her, Sarah's thumb hovered over her father's name in her phone's contact list.

Laughter fluttered down the hallway. It was five days before Christmas—three until the bakery was supposed to open—and Sophia was keeping Ginny company as she made a few last-minute tweaks to the recipes she anticipated being most popular. Her sister's optimism amazed Sarah, especially given that they still had no plan to have the ordinance changed before opening day. But Ginny trusted God to come through if it were meant to be, so Sarah was trying to follow her lead.

Sarah's heart beat erratic thumps against her chest. She longed to join the women in the kitchen, but first she needed to call Father. Gathering her courage, she dialed.

The phone rang three times before he answered. "Nice to finally hear from you, Sarah." His words dripped with condescension.

"Hey, Dad." Yes, Dad—not Father.

She was taking back the authority he had over her life.

"I'm looking forward to seeing you this week." In the background, the click of keys sounded. It was Sunday evening in England, so sometime in the early afternoon in Boston. He must be at work, as usual. "Your mother has outdone herself for this year's Christmas Eve soiree. It will be the talk of the town, I'm sure."

Here went nothing. "Actually, that's what I was calling about." A pause while she swallowed. "I am not going to be able to make it back after all. Ginny's bakery is set to open, but there have been some difficulties—"

"What kind of difficulties?" Had she imagined it or did he actually sound concerned? "And what does that have to do with you keeping your word?"

Or not.

OK, so staying longer wasn't just about Ginny. It was about Sarah too. She had no desire to return yet. There was so much left to explore here. With Ginny. And yes, with Michael. In the three days since she and Michael had visited the lighthouse, they'd been together almost nonstop in the evenings. Things between them had stayed friendly, but something new hovered there. Something that Sarah longed to explore despite all the odds stacked against them when it came to having any sort of romantic relationship.

Not that she was going to tell Father—er, Dad— any of that. Sarah pulled herself upright. He didn't hold power over her anymore. She was an adult, and she was his daughter too. Dad needed to respect her. But if she never stood up for herself and did things her own way, he never would.

And if he decided to follow through on his threat and pull funding from New Dawn, then Melissa was right. They'd find a way to keep it going.

"I realize that you might be disappointed, but we can celebrate together when I return."

"What about Warren?"

Poor Warren. He'd gotten in the middle of all this, and that wasn't his fault. "I called him yesterday and let him know that I needed to cancel our date." He'd been so understanding and sweet, albeit concerned. She'd tried to let him down gently by explaining that she needed more time in England and that when she returned, she'd be happy to meet up as friends. Emphasis on "friends."

He had been quiet afterward, but she'd expected that.

Her father harrumphed. "I don't like this one bit,

Sarah. It sounds as if your sister has been a poor influence on you."

"Don't blame Ginny for this, Dad. I have my own mind, and I'm finally using it." Well, that had come out a bit harsh. She blinked slowly as she focused on softening her tone. "I love you and will miss seeing you for the holidays. Please let Mom know that I'll buy her a fabulous gift while I'm here."

"I'll tell her you won't be at her party, and it will crush her."

She eased out a breath through her teeth. "Well, I'd better go. I'll call you guys on Christmas."

"Just when do you plan to be home? I won't be able to give you vacation time off work indefinitely, you know."

"I'll be back in the office on January 2. I called to make sure Thomas can cover for me the extra week. Nothing ever happens between Christmas and New Year's anyway."

And with that, the phone went dead. "Real mature, Dad." Sarah sighed.

Oh well. Her part was done and she hadn't felt this free in a long time. Hopping off the bed, she set her phone onto the side table and strolled down the hallway toward the kitchen.

Sophia sat on the counter-height stool while Ginny glazed cinnamon buns. They stopped their conversation and focused on Sarah, expectation heavy in their eyes.

"Well?" Ginny licked the spatula and set it in the kitchen sink. "How did it go?"

She'd asked her sister and Sophia to pray while she'd called Dad. "About as well as could be expected. But I'm still standing, right?" She walked over to the pan in front of Ginny, pulled a large sliver off the corner bun, and shoved it into her mouth. Light and decadent and just what the doctor ordered.

"No fair," Sophia said. "My baby has been dying for one of those buns since they came out of the oven. Hand one over before I go all mama bear on you both."

They laughed and Ginny took out some plates and dished a bun onto each. Then they gathered at the small table by the window to relax. A soft snow had started falling earlier today and was supposed to continue off and on until Christmas. Apparently it was rare to get it this early in Cornwall, but some said that last year's weather had started a new trend.

"So. Inquiring minds want to know." Sophia slid a fork into her roll, slicing it down the middle. "What's going on with you and a certain local photographer?"

"Oh yes, inquiring minds *do* want to know that." Ginny flashed Sarah a pointed look and saucy smile as she twirled her fork in the air.

So this was what an ambush felt like. Sarah stabbed her roll. "Nothing is going on." That didn't mean she had no interest . . . but did Michael? He'd flirted, sure, and he'd been an amazing friend. But he hadn't said anything so far that had led her to believe he wanted any sort of romantic relationship with her.

And that probably made him the smarter of the two, given that her life was in Boston and his was here.

At Sophia's snort, Ginny laughed. Then they all dissolved into giggles. What were they, middle schoolers?

But she had to admit it felt good to laugh. Things had been far too tense as of late, and Sarah had allowed circumstances to shadow her joy and zest for life, for the things she cared about. That was something else she'd discovered during the last several days in spending time with Michael. He had this infectious happiness, this optimism, despite his struggles.

He'd confided to her that he was expected to go into the family business but that he'd much rather pursue his photography instead. And while his parents weren't anything like hers, a sense of family obligation pulled him to stay in Port Willis.

Even still, he remained positive about the future.

"Just know we don't believe you one bit. And we've both been exactly where you are." All teasing aside, Sophia watched her with knowing eyes lit with compassion.

Ginny nodded. "And also know that you two are about as cute as cherry pie. Oh, or cupcake ice cream cones. And of course, my personal favorite, chocolate-glazed donut cookies."

Sarah rolled her eyes. "I believe the title of World's Cutest Couple goes to you and Steven."

A blush crept across Ginny's cheeks. "And to think I almost missed it."

What if Sarah left for Boston and never told Michael how she felt about him? Would she regret it forever? The idea equally terrified and electrified her insides. She pushed the remainder of her roll around her plate, sticky cinnamon filling trailing behind.

Wow, OK, she really needed to shift her thoughts away from romance. Sarah cleared her throat. "Has anyone heard anything else from Rebecca Trengrouse?" The woman had been a veritable ghost since the council meeting. Of course, it wasn't like Sarah was frequenting Trengrouse Bakery much these days, but it was strange to have not seen her around town either.

The change in subject seemed to catch Ginny off guard. Her shoulders drooped. "Not a word. I tried to stop by a few days ago, but the bakery had shut down early. When Mr. Trengrouse ran things, he stayed open until 5:00 p.m. sharp every day. But I guess it *is* right before the holidays. Maybe Rebecca wants to spend some time with him, especially if he's as sick as she seems to imply."

Something niggled at the back of Sarah's mind. "Haven't you seen him recently?"

"No one has. Not that I know of, anyway." Ginny set down her fork and leaned back in her seat.

"You're right." Sophia rubbed her stomach, eyes squinting in concentration. "I haven't seen him in a long time. He hasn't been at church for more than a month. I saw him just before Thanksgiving. Remember, he brought all those pastries for the baskets we made up for the less fortunate? But that's the last time from what I can recall."

An idea sparked but Sarah needed more information before it could fully ignite. "Are he and his daughter close?"

Sophia stood, gathering up the ladies' plates. "I'm not sure. Gin? You've lived here longer than me."

"I don't know much about her, but Steven said Mr. Trengrouse was always a bit gruff around the edges. Apparently he had pretty high expectations for Rebecca and her younger brother." Ginny joined Sophia at the sink and took one of the plates from her friend's hand, flicked on the faucet, and ran the dish under the water. "But ever since his wife died a few years ago, he's really softened up."

Hmmm. So maybe the plan forming in Sarah's brain wouldn't work. Then again, it might.

And she wasn't above a Hail Mary right about now, especially for Ginny's sake.

Sarah stood. "Be right back." She headed for her room, grabbed her phone, and shot up a prayer as she composed a text to Michael.

Sarah: *You up for a rescue mission tomorrow?*

Michael: *Sure. I'm off work at four. Who are we rescuing?*

Sarah: *Not who. What. And the answer is Ginny's bakery.*

Michael: *I'm in.*

Sarah sent him a thumbs up emoji, closed her messages, and pushed away any lingering romantic thoughts. Whatever feelings she had for Michael were nothing compared to the adrenaline coursing through her veins.

Tomorrow, she would save her sister's bakery.

CHAPTER 11

"Do you think this will work?" Sarah studied the front of the quaint stone cottage situated against a hillside overlooking Port Willis. Turning, she could see the harbor, the shops, the week-of-Christmas crowds bustling about. Up here, out of the main part of town, the stress had the potential to melt away.

How ironic then, that hers was at an all-time high.

This was her last shot at helping Ginny open her bakery on time.

Michael nudged open the wooden gate surrounding the property and beckoned for her to go ahead of him. "I'm not sure but we have to try. I can't believe we didn't think of it sooner."

"Same here." She stepped through, her boots

crunching some dead fallen leaves from the tree in the front yard.

Though the sun had shown almost all day, sporadic cloud cover that threatened more snow dimmed the last vestiges of sunlight. None of what had fallen so far had stuck, but that didn't make it any less magical. Sarah had tried to force herself to enjoy the peaceful flutter, but her head—and her heart—had been so full of other thoughts.

They arrived at the front door, and Sarah's fingers tingled. "Here goes nothing."

She knocked.

The door opened quicker than she expected, almost as if the house's occupant had been sitting by the front window in anticipation of visitors. Sarah squinted to see into the dimly lit home, but finally her eyes focused on a stooped man in his seventies with a white beard and round eyeglasses perched on the end of his nose.

"Mr. Trengrouse?"

"Yes?" He took another step outside, stopping under the light cast by a wrought-iron lamp on the other side of the gate.

"Hi, I'm Sarah Bentley and this is Michael Ham—"

"I know Michael. How are you?"

Michael cleared his throat. "I'm good, sir. It's been some time since I've seen you."

"Not that long. Wasn't it just last week that you

stole a peppermint stick from my counter?" Though his words could be interpreted in several different ways, his tone left his meaning clear. The lazy smile that spread across his face also clarified his teasing.

With a laugh, Michael shook Mr. Trengrouse's hand. "Not last week but perhaps last month." His expression grew more serious. "How are you, Mr. Trengrouse?"

The older man waved a hand. "I'm fine, fine. I've had a wet cough and something about walking pneumonia, but you know nothing will keep me down long." He turned to Sarah. "I've heard tale that you're Ginny Rose's sister."

"Yes, sir." His hawkish eyes pierced her—as if they could discern more than he was saying. She gulped. "And that's actually what we've come to talk with you about. My sister. And her bakery."

"Ah, the opening is rather soon, is it not? I'm trying to convince Rebecca to let me go, but she keeps insisting my doctor wouldn't be on board with me getting out just yet." A warm smile brightened his face. "You know daughters. Much too overprotective." A cough fell from his drooping lips, enveloping his body in fits for a few moments. "Pardon me."

Michael exchanged a glance with Sarah. They'd agreed that he should do most of the talking since he had a relationship with the man—or, at the very least, wasn't a complete stranger. "Mr. Trengrouse, would you mind if we come inside for a moment?"

The man's scrutinizing gaze fell on Michael. "I suppose that's all right. Come along."

Sarah and Michael followed Mr. Trengrouse to a green couch that had seen better days. The house smelled of cinnamon and flour. Did Mr. Trengrouse still bake? How would that be, to no longer be able to do the thing you loved? Although if he'd been honest with Ginny, he seemed to be looking forward to retirement.

Michael assisted the older man in lowering himself into a worn chair boasting an indent of its favorite recipient then joined Sarah on the couch.

"Now, what is all this seriousness about? It's almost Christmas, you know." Mr. Trengrouse folded his hands over his paunch of a stomach and leaned back against the overstuffed seat.

Sarah bit the inside of her cheek. What a nice Christmas present for Ginny this would be if she and Michael could pull it off.

Even though they'd discussed him taking the lead, one glance at Michael indicated he was waiting on her. His hand found Sarah's fingers, tucked them inside—a reminder that he was here, whatever she needed.

Sarah took a deep breath. "Sir, my sister's bakery isn't going to open."

The man's wry gray eyebrows launched up. "Whatever do you mean?"

"The parish council that oversees Port Willis

won't allow it. Because of your daughter." Sarah launched into an explanation of the situation, trying to keep her tone from wandering into accusation and staying focused on the facts. That part was more difficult than she'd thought.

As Mr. Trengrouse listened, his face and shoulders sagged. "You'll have to forgive Rebecca. She's a good girl and she means well, but ever since her mother died . . ." His eyes wandered to the fireplace mantel where a portrait of his family hung. "She couldn't wait to get out of Port Willis when she turned eighteen, so I didn't expect her to want the bakery when I retired. Her brother certainly doesn't. But now that Rebecca is back, I can see she's afraid of losing it. Perhaps she's holding on out of fear."

While Sarah couldn't relate to wanting any part of her family's inheritance, she most certainly understood allowing fear to run one's life and making decisions because of it. "We have no problem at all with her continuing to run your bakery. I know for a fact that Ginny purposefully is planning a menu that doesn't conflict with any of your most popular items out of respect for you both." She leaned forward, gripping Michael's hand tighter than she'd intended. "But sir, do you think that you could talk Rebecca out of having this ordinance enforced? There is still time to turn it around if we work quickly."

Brow furrowed, Mr. Trengrouse flicked the edge

of his nose with his thumb. After a few moments of contemplation, he nodded. "Yes, of course. Ginny is far too talented and has put too much into this to allow her to go under." He straightened as if forcing the resolve through his whole body. "I will talk with Rebecca when she returns home tonight. And if she protests, I will contact the council myself and sign whatever document needed to allow this ordinance to be dismissed."

"Really?"

At Sarah's jubilant response, Michael threw his arm around her shoulders and squeezed. "Thank you, sir. We appreciate this so much."

We. That had a nice ring to it.

With a kiss to his weathered cheek, Sarah thanked Mr. Trengrouse and followed Michael out the door, out the gate, and down the path to the edge of the nearest bluff heading back into town. Snow had begun to fall once more, creating a beautiful mosaic of white against the darkening sky, with lights from the villages twinkling below and dim moonlight falling from above.

Before they could go any farther, she stopped and launched herself into Michael's arms. "We did it!"

His arms came around her, hugging her and lifting Sarah off her feet. "*You* did it. And were quite brilliant, I may add." He set her down and pulled back to look at her.

The heat from his gaze nearly warmed her

enough to forget about the snowflakes falling on their lashes and cheeks. Her toes curled. "Thank you all the same for being here."

"Always." He moved his hand from her waist, and it lingered near her face, his fingers skimming her cheek as if he didn't know what to do with them—what to do with this moment stretching between them, one instant yet a thousand just the same.

But Sarah knew. Even as Michael's hand dropped back to her waist, she summoned her courage. "So, I've been meaning to tell you. I'm not leaving on Wednesday night."

"You're not?"

She shook her head. "I'm staying for another week."

"That's great." His words fell flat—and so did her heart. Did he not want her to stay? Had she misinterpreted things?

But whatever the case, she needed to tell him how she felt, or she'd always regret it. No, she didn't know how things would ever work between them or if they ever would, but she was free of her father now.

She finally had the luxury of finding out for herself.

With trembling fingers, Sarah lightly cupped Michael's cheeks. He didn't take his eyes from hers, but even in the dim light, his question burned.

She'd answer it as best she could. "I want more

time with you, plain and simple." Then she rose on her heeled boots and captured his mouth with hers.

For a moment, he stood frozen. But then his hands tightened around her, pulling Sarah closer as his lips explored hers, first a gentle touch then with fervent emotion. Sarah melted against him, into him, as if she'd always belonged there.

Maybe she had.

At long last, the kiss ended. Sarah sighed as she snuggled against him and looked out over the ocean. Snow wet her hair, and a tiny shiver ran up her spine—but if it were weather or kiss induced, who could tell?

"In case it wasn't clear, I want more time with you as well." Michael's voice rumbled in his chest.

They both laughed and she tapped him on the arm with the back of her hand. He snatched it and pulled off her glove. Then he kissed the tip of each finger slowly, lighting a fire in Sarah's toes until she couldn't do anything but turn and kiss him again.

Finally, he squeezed her waist. "I think we'd better get you back to your sister so you can tell her the great news."

"About this?" Sarah moved a finger back and forth between them, grinning.

"What else would I be talking about?"

Joining hands, they meandered back into the heart of town, chatting about plans for the next week. "I'd love for you to join us for supper on Christmas Day."

She'd met his parents, sister, brother-in-law, and niece in passing, but a holiday together? Wow. "Um, OK. If you're sure."

"I am."

All right, then.

As they drew closer to Ginny's place, the snow stopped. A light was on in the kitchen. Huh. Ginny was supposed to be at the bakery until late tonight. Maybe her plans had changed.

Sarah turned to Michael and hooked her arms around his neck. "I don't want to go inside. But I promised Melissa I'd do a few things online tonight."

"And I'd better get started on my Christmas shopping."

She shook her head. "Figures."

"I'm sure you've had yours done for a long time." He pressed his forehead against hers, his grin teasing.

"November, to be exact." Of course, now she needed to shop for one person she hadn't anticipated . . .

Nothing about this had been expected.

"That's adorable." Michael leaned in and brushed his lips against hers. The kiss ended far too soon.

She was just about to pull him back in for another when the door opened behind them, flooding the spot where they stood with light. Turning, she blinked against the glare to find a figure standing in the doorway.

"Sarah?"

Her hands fell from Michael's shoulders as she squinted. "Warren?"

CHAPTER 12

"*H*i, Sarah."

It took her brain a few moments to catch up with her eyes. Warren Kensington stood outside Ginny's door, hands crossed over his gray cashmere sweater, a strange look shadowing his face. "What are you doing here?"

Warren shifted from one foot to another. "I came to see you."

Obviously. But why? She'd tried to be clear on the phone about their status as just friends.

Michael cleared his throat and, with one arm still tucked firmly around Sarah's waist, extended his free hand toward Warren. "Michael Hammett. Pleasure to meet you."

Eyeing the placement of Michael's other arm, Warren shook his hand. "Warren Kensington. Sarah's . . . friend from Boston."

The men lowered their hands and turned toward Sarah. "Why don't we get out of this cold?" She stepped forward and out of Michael's embrace, but as she crossed the home's threshold, Warren put out his hand to block Michael.

"Hey, man, I'd love to chat with Sarah alone for a minute if you don't mind?"

Goodness. She'd never known Warren to be this rude. But it must have been a surprise for him to find her embracing some other guy less than a month after they'd gone on their perfectly pleasant date, so she supposed she'd give him a pass, especially if he'd witnessed their kiss.

The firm line of Michael's lips drooped, and his gaze found hers. "What would you like, Sarah?"

Just the fact he asked made her want to kiss him again. But it was probably easier to deal with the Warren situation—to get to the heart of why he was here—if it were just the two of them. "I'll call you, OK? Soon."

It seemed like the logical choice, but when she saw the way his jaw tightened, the fake smile he forced, it seemed her brain had perhaps led her astray. "Sure. Yeah. I'll see you." And without another word, he turned and walked away into the darkness.

She wanted to rush after him, explain her thoughts, her reasons for wanting to be alone with Warren. But she'd do that later.

Warren shut the door and tapped the doorknob a

few times before rotating toward Sarah. He cocked his head. "Sorry about that. I know I was impolite. It's just . . . I took a few red eyes to get here and haven't slept much. And well, I . . ."

Now that she studied him, his eyes did look a bit bloodshot, his hair more tousled than usual. Poor man. She approached him and squeezed his forearm. "It's fine." A pause weighted the space between them. "How are you?"

As if waiting for an invitation, Warren leaned into a hug, and his mandarin orange, black pepper, and lavender cologne enveloped her. It was a pleasant scent—maybe even an enjoyable one—but it didn't draw her in like it might have once.

Warren held on, perhaps for a moment too long, but finally released her. "So, you're probably wondering why I'm here."

"I'm guessing you're not just in the neighborhood." She attempted a weak laugh.

He didn't even crack a smile. "Not exactly. Can we sit?" He gestured toward the couch, and they headed that way. "I hope you don't mind that your sister let me in. She had to run back to the bakery but said I was welcome to wait for you here."

Both sank onto the couch, and Sarah turned her body slightly to face him before realizing too late that this position left their knees touching. Warren placed his left arm along the back of the couch and reached his other toward her hands, which she'd folded in her lap. His serious eyes studied her for a minute before he spoke. "I'm just going to come out and say it, if it isn't obvious. I like you, Sarah. A lot. More than anyone I've ever dated. You're intelligent, caring, and passionate. And I didn't like the way we left things on the phone the other night."

His Adam's apple slid up and down his throat.

Her stomach constricted at the sight. "Warren—"

"Let me finish, please." At her nod, he continued. "I know you think I only pursued you because of your father's urging, and that may have been what prompted me at first—but only because I assumed you'd never date someone like me."

"Are you kidding? You're the kind one, Warren, and that's a rarity. I'm sorry I let my family stuff get in between us. That wasn't fair to you."

"No, I get it." With his free hand, he played with a piece of Sarah's hair as he spoke. Though a bit beyond friendly, the gesture didn't freak her out. Something about Warren just put her at ease, even if her veins didn't catch fire with him near. "I guess I just wanted to let you know I'm still here. And to make some sort of grand gesture or something. Maybe that was idiotic of me." A pause. "Or maybe I'm too late."

So he *had* seen the kiss she'd shared with Michael. "That's sweet of you, Warren." And if she'd never met Michael, then maybe she and Warren could go back home and see where things led—see if this comfort, this friendship, could develop into stronger, more passionate feelings.

But she *had* met Michael, and now she'd compare everyone to him.

"As for being too late . . ." She squeezed his hand again. "I'm sorry. I didn't mean to hurt you."

He tacked on a sad smile. "I understand." He extricated his hands with a gentle pull then placed them into his lap. "Guess I'd better get out of your hair."

"Don't be silly. Stay. Cornwall is beautiful this time of year." Yes, that would make things a bit awkward, but he'd come all this way.

His look told her exactly what he thought of that plan. "I'll stay the night but head out tomorrow." He stood and she followed suit. "Oh, that reminds me." He picked up his jacket, which he'd draped over the arm of the couch, and dug in the pocket, producing a sealed envelope. "This is for you."

"You wrote me a letter?"

"No. Your father did. I promised I'd deliver it to you."

"He knew you were coming?" At Warren's glance, she held up her hand. "Who am I kidding? Of course he did."

Warren threw on his jacket, leaned in, and kissed her cheek. "If you happen to change your mind, I'll be at the B&B around the corner."

She hugged him and he left. Then she snagged a

kitchen knife, cut open the envelope flap, and sank onto a counter stool to read the letter, which, of course, was typed on her father's official letterhead.

Sarah,

Doubtless by now you will have seen Warren and heard him out. I hope you give him a chance. Whatever you may think of me, I do want you to be happy, and I feel he is the right sort of man to do that. However, if you see things differently, then perhaps we can discuss some alternative solutions to encourage the merger with his father's company.

I'm sorry that you seem to feel the best way to spend Christmas is away from your mother and me—and that it's likely my own fault. I pushed you with all my expectations. I never meant to be overbearing. I merely see greatness in you. You have the fortitude and commitment your siblings lack, and I trust no one more than you to run my company when I am gone.

That being said, this experiment of yours—running away to England, just as Virginia did, manipulating me to get what you want—doesn't sit well with me. I do not appreciate my loyalty and love being tested in this way.

You have a choice, and the ball, so to speak, is in your court, Sarah. Come home for Christmas and all will be forgiven.

Father

PS: I recently spoke with a good friend of mine, Jeff

Gentry, and he's informed me that your charity is representing his wife in a nasty case that spreads all sorts of malicious rumors about him. As your main donor, I insist that you look more closely into this case. I'm sure we can all come to some sort of agreement that will be best for everyone involved. I'd hate to have to pull my funding, but I cannot have my name tied to anything untoward. You understand, I'm sure, my dear.

Sarah's hand trembled as she crushed the paper into a ball. A sob rose from deep in her chest. So this is what it had come to. Father was never going to let her have her own life. Deep down she'd always known it, even though she'd hoped that standing up for herself would change things.

But it didn't matter how good of a daughter she was, how much she loved him, how much she sacrificed.

He would always win.

Because there was no way she could stay in Cornwall, wiling away the week with Michael, now that Father had threatened New Dawn. She knew without a doubt that if she didn't get back there and fight him on the Jeff Gentry issue, New Dawn would be no more. Not only would he pull his funding, he'd find a way to drive it into the ground, into dust.

All of this—Cornwall, Michael, her time with Ginny—had been a lovely Christmas dream. Nothing more.

After the opening of Ginny's bakery, Sarah would

return to her role of dutiful daughter. Although this time, she wouldn't sacrifice everything. Not her faith. And not New Dawn. She'd fight for Elise Gentry, no matter what her father said.

Where she worked and who she dated, well, those weren't as important as making sure that her life's work wasn't overturned, that others were protected. Her father might never love or respect Sarah the way she'd hoped he would, but by committing her life to serving others, at least one Father would be proud.

$\mathcal{M}$aking a decision one day and following through the next had never been so difficult.

Sarah braced herself against the wind blowing upward from the harbor as she made her way down High Street. The bright, cloudless sky disguised the bitter cold that only showed itself when she huffed and her breath became visible.

The weather that, just yesterday, felt magical mocked her today.

She'd already informed her sister about her change in plans. Sarah had even texted Warren and let him know she'd be flying back tomorrow night. It was only fair, since he had come all this way to see her.

But now she needed to tell Michael.

Her legs threatened to give out on her after a full

night of pacing. At four-something in the morning, Ginny had finally interrupted her brooding, and the two had talked at length. But despite Ginny's attempts to bolster Sarah and encourage her to live her own life, Sarah knew that the only way to move forward was to move backward.

Which, of course, had led to more pacing. Because how discouraging was *that*?

As she made her way to meet Michael in their spot on the grassy bluff above the harbor, Sarah was so lost in thought that she nearly missed someone calling her name.

She halted and turned her head. Trengrouse Bakery stood just across the way. And there was Rebecca Trengrouse, waving at her and shouting for her to stop.

Did the woman want to chew her out for meddling by talking with her father yesterday? Oh, who cared anymore? Let her come. Sarah waited while Rebecca crossed the street, her arms pumping before wrapping tightly around her chest as she approached. "Thanks for stopping."

"It seemed important." Sarah eyed her. The woman must be freezing without a jacket on. "Do you want to go inside?"

"This won't take long."

Here we go. "All right."

Instead of straightening to her full height in true Rebecca fashion, her shoulders drooped under

Sarah's scrutiny. "I just wanted to let you know that, as per my father's wishes, I've spoken with the parish council and agreed to bypass the ordinance. Your sister can open her bakery as planned."

Sarah bit her cheek to keep from saying what she really thought of Rebecca's "generosity." The important thing was Ginny's dream could continue forward as planned. "Great." She paused, forcing the next words from her mouth. "Thank you."

Rebecca's feet shuffled against the cobblestone, and she stared at the ground.

Sarah quirked an eyebrow. "Was there something else?"

"It's just . . ." Rebecca bounced on the balls of her feet. "I'm sorry, all right? I got a bit overzealous and, well, I guess that I just thought if I kept the family business going, maybe things would change. Maybe I'd finally have a good relationship with my father. Maybe I'd finally . . . be happy." She blew a blond strand of hair out of her eyes. "Sorry, I don't know why I'm telling you all this. The point is, I was wrong and I'm sorry for the trouble I've caused."

For the first time since meeting her, Sarah didn't completely despise Rebecca Trengrouse. Like Michael had suggested, perhaps she and Rebecca were more alike than Sarah cared to admit. Still . . . "You should tell that to Ginny, not me."

The woman nodded. "I will." She turned and headed back to the bakery.

Mr. Trengrouse had come through, and Sarah would indeed be leaving Ginny with her bakery intact. Even if her own dreams had fallen to pieces around her, at least she'd managed to do something right while in Cornwall.

Heaving a sigh—of relief, of trepidation?—Sarah turned and continued her march toward the harbor. Calm waters lapped inside the quay, but beyond it the wind skimmed the top of the sea. She climbed the path to the cliff overlooking the waters and found Michael standing near the edge, embracing the breeze.

Whatever came after this, she'd try to shove it from her memory. *This* is how she'd choose to remember him.

A few pieces of gravel tumbled down the path as she walked, alerting him to her presence, and the smile on his face as he turned toward her stabbed her insides.

"Hey there, gorgeous." In seconds, he was hugging her and leaning down for a kiss. How natural it felt.

And Sarah, God help her, let Michael hold her. If this was going to be the end, she needed to soak up all the warmth from their last moments together.

Don't cry, don't cry. Don't ruin this.

But she couldn't fake her emotions anymore, and soon, tears came faster than she could swipe them away.

Michael pulled back, hands on her upper arms, a look of alarm replacing the smile. "What's wrong, love?"

"Everything." A fresh torrent of tears sprang from her eyes.

He held her again, not saying anything. Eventually, he led her to a huge blanket he'd laid on the ground. They sat down and wrapped it up and over their shoulders and backs, enclosing it around them, cocooning their warmth.

How pathetic she was—about to end things with him yet accepting the comfort he gave. She had to tell him so he'd stop being so wonderful.

Sarah finally removed her head from his shoulder and sat up, using the blanket to dry her eyes. Clearing her throat, she chanced a look at Michael.

The space between his brows had narrowed, and his eyes questioned her. "You're leaving tomorrow, aren't you?"

How did he . . . "Y-yes." The word croaked in her throat. "After Ginny's opening. As originally planned."

"Was it something I did?"

"No!" She fumbled under the blanket until she found his hand. "You were perfect. It was all . . . perfect. Just not meant to be."

He looked like he wanted to ask why, but instead he turned and gazed at the horizon. Wasn't he going to fight her on this? Scream at her? She surely deserved it for jerking him around.

But as they sat there holding hands and watching the ocean beat the rocks in the distance, realization settled upon her. He was doing the one thing no other man in her life had ever done for her.

He was accepting her decision.

Which made this the best and the worst moment of her life.

CHAPTER 14

How was she ever going to go home after this?

Sarah stopped moving for just a moment to catch her breath. Her feet and lower back ached from a full morning and afternoon of constant movement, but every step had been worth it. Sarah's eyes roamed Ginny's bakery from her place in the corner. All day customers had streamed in and out. At times, like now, there was a line out the door and every seat was filled.

Customers still padded in, shaking off loose snow from their boots onto Ginny's welcome mat. The weather had finally caught up with Sarah's emotions, painting the sky a dark gray.

William, Sophia, and Steven took turns behind the registry—though both men made sure Sophia didn't stand for too long—while Ginny and Sarah restocked the shelves and greeted guests. Two of Sophia's employees manned the bookstore so Sophia could be here for Ginny's big day.

Sarah watched as her sister patted a vaguely familiar elderly man's arm and laughed with him. Who was he? The man grabbed his cane from the table where he'd sat to eat his baked good. Ah, yes. He was the older gentleman from Trengrouse Bakery, the one Rebecca Trengrouse had treated so terribly.

Good you for, Gin.

As if she'd heard Sarah's thoughts, Ginny looked up at her and grinned. She said goodbye to the man and walked toward Sarah. "I still can't believe these people gave up some of their day to be here and encourage me."

Sarah slipped her arm around Ginny's back as they watched the crowd eating and enjoying. Classic rock music played on low in the background. The door between the bakery and the bookstore stood wide open, and guests trickled back and forth exactly as Gin and Sophia had intended. "They're not just here to encourage you, though I do think many of them love you very much." The words caught in Sarah's throat. Goodness, she had been emotional the last few days. "But you've opened an amazing bakery, with delicious treats that are going to become fast favorites. You'd better start hiring some employees to help out, you know."

"I plan to, once I know the sales volume can support it." Ginny chewed her bottom lip. "Sarah, I understand why you're leaving, but I wish . . ."

"I know." Sarah laid her head against Ginny's. "I'm so extremely proud of you, little sis."

"And I'm proud of you."

She shouldn't be, but Sarah wouldn't ruin a perfectly good moment by saying so. "Don't think that just because I'm leaving that it'll be years before you see me again. I have plans to visit this summer." She hoped by then that she and Father would have worked out whatever was between them so she could take off the time without feeling guilty.

"I'm going to hold you to that."

"You'd better." Who knew what would happen by then? Between her and Father . . . or her and Warren. Her gaze swiveled to the corner of the bakery. Warren had been stationed there for most of the day, welcoming newcomers and handing out menus Steven had designed.

When Sarah had decided to leave, Warren had kept his original travel plans. He'd claimed it was easier than rescheduling, but Sarah couldn't help but wonder if the real reason was so he could spend an extra day with her. Instead of trying to persuade her to reconsider dating him or sightseeing together, he'd rolled up his Gucci sleeves and helped her and Ginny put the finishing touches on the bakery last night.

Even Sarah had to admit that she'd been surprised. Most senior-level executives weren't willing to dirty their hands—literally speaking, at least.

"He's not a bad guy, you know."

Sarah started. Ginny had caught her staring at Warren. "I never said he was." He just wasn't Michael. But Michael wasn't in the picture anymore. He hadn't even stopped by yet today. Maybe he was just working.

Or maybe she'd broken his heart.

All she knew was her own would never be the same.

"Just make sure you don't settle. That's not fair to anyone."

"I know, Gin." And she did.

"I'd better get back to it." Ginny hugged Sarah and flitted off to work the register for a while. Side by side, she and Steven made quite the team.

As Sarah bussed a few newly emptied tables—sometimes scrubbing much harder than necessary—the hairs on the back of her neck prickled and she glanced up.

Michael stood in the doorway, his gaze on her mournful. He tugged the beanie from his head and ran a hand through his curls. Then, as if ripping Velcro, he maneuvered his eyes toward the register, plastered a smile on his face, and headed toward Ginny, shouting his congratulations.

Sarah turned back to the table and pushed the wet rag in her hand across the table so hard that her upper arm vibrated.

A few minutes later, the music quieted. "Excuse me, everyone?" Ginny's voice filled the room from where she stood in front of the register. All eyes, including Sarah's, turned to face her sister.

"I just wanted to say thank you so much for all of your support today." Ginny's lips quivered as she took the time to look at each person, lingering longer on William, Sophia, Sarah, and—of course—Steven, who stood off to the side only feet away from her. "There was a time when I didn't know where I belonged. When I let everyone else tell me my worth and allowed others to define me. This bakery is a culmination of so many things for me, but ultimately, it's a homecoming. It's like the perfect marriage of cinnamon rolls and icing. Of spaghetti sauce and noodles. Of . . . well, you understand."

The crowd laughed but Sarah worked to keep tears from spilling down her cheeks.

Ginny took the few steps toward Steven and held out her hand. "I couldn't have done it without each and every one of you, but most especially this man right here. He's been incredibly supportive through all of the ups and downs." Then she got down on one knee. "And speaking of marriage . . ."

Now a quick gasp and several *ahhhs* flew from all

directions. Was Ginny doing what they all thought she was doing?

But before she could say another word, Steven lowered himself to the ground as well, so they were once again face-to-face. "What do you think you're doing?"

"Asking you to marry me, silly."

Steven snorted as he reached into the back pocket of his jeans and pulled something from it. When he opened his palm, a diamond ring winked under the bakery's lights.

Ginny put her hands to her mouth and her eyes widened. "What's that for?"

"Before you jumped the gun, I was planning to ask you the same question tonight." He slid the ring onto Ginny's trembling finger. "So, Ginny Rose, will you make me the happiest man alive and marry me?"

"Yes!" Ginny threw her arms around Steven's neck and kissed him.

Oh, Gin.

Now Sarah really was crying. The bell above the bakery's door jingled and she turned to see Michael's retreating back.

Beside the door, Warren stood taking in the scene. He caught her eye and smiled.

Sarah swung her gaze back to the happy couple and brushed the tears from her cheeks as she moved forward to congratulate them.

AS HORRIBLE AS the goodbyes had been, it was the hellos Sarah dreaded most. She shuddered as she imagined the look of satisfaction on Father's face when he saw her walk into the Christmas Eve party tomorrow night.

"Are you cold?" Warren unwound his scarf as they waited in line at Cornwall Airport Newquay to check their bags.

"I'm fine, thanks." In fact, it was actually rather hot inside the airport, probably from the combined body heat of all these people pressed together—a phenomenon for such a tiny place.

Sarah flicked her passport back and forth against her palm. Could this line be any slower? "I'll bet you're wishing you'd left earlier." Two days before Christmas certainly wasn't the best day to travel.

"I'm right where I want to be."

Oh, how she wished she could force herself to feel weak in the knees at his sweet statement. "Warren—"

"Sarah Bentley, is that you, my dear?"

She turned at the kind voice to find Mavis Lincoln looking at her. "Hi, Mrs. Lincoln. What are you doing here?"

The woman didn't have any suitcases with her, just a small purse slung across her shoulder. Funny. Sarah had pictured the owner of an antique shop carrying something oversized and vintage. "I was just making my way back to the waiting area when I saw you. I'm here for my nephew and his wife. Their flight was supposed to come in last night but got bumped to this evening."

"Oliver and Joy, right?" At Mavis's nod, Sarah turned to Warren and made introductions. "We're headed home in time for my parents' Christmas party tomorrow night."

Mavis eyed Warren, a smile at odds with the crease of curiosity on her forehead. "I am glad you were able to stay for your sister's opening. I stopped in first thing, and I know it's going to be a raving success. I'm only sorry Joy and Oliver won't make it."

Warren and Sarah advanced in the line. Mavis took a step to follow them but winced at the movement.

That's right, she had gout. Why had her family sent her to the airport to fetch her nephew? Sarah glanced at Warren. "Would you mind getting my suitcase checked in?"

"Not at all."

"Thanks." Sarah slipped under the rope dividing the lines, and took Mrs. Lincoln's elbow. "May I sit with you for a few minutes?"

"That would be lovely." The woman shuffled toward a bank of chairs in the main terminal area with Sarah beside her in case she needed assistance. They wound their way across the crowded floor until arriving at a pair of empty seats.

Mavis grunted as she lowered herself. The woman's cheeks appeared flushed. "Thank you, dear."

Sarah sat between her and a teenage boy glued to his phone. "Of course."

Grasping Sarah's hand in her knobby red one, Mavis tilted her head. "Now, just who is that handsome young man to you?"

"Warren? Oh. He's . . . complicated." Sarah looked away. The windows facing the tarmac were smudged from the cold. A child stood there next to his mother, pointing and exclaiming about the planes and their lights in the dark.

"Complicated is right. From what I saw, I thought one of our locals had perhaps caught your eye."

Michael. Even just thinking his name pricked Sarah's eyes with hot tears. "Perhaps one did. But he's not the practical choice."

"What does practicality have to do with love?"

Sarah whipped her gaze back toward Mavis. The temperature in the overly warm room seemed to drop. "If you're my father? Everything."

"And are you your father?" The tip of Mavis's nose shone.

"No. But he wants me to be. Or, at least, to obey him. In his eyes, that's the only time I'm useful." Sarah sighed, rubbing her temple with her free hand.

"It's a long story, but suffice it to say, I've given up trying to please him. The only one I'm interested in pleasing now is God. So I'm going back, leaving all this, leaving a good man, to keep fighting the good fight."

Mavis was quiet for a moment as she studied Sarah. "Usefulness is quite an interesting subject and one I'm well acquainted with. One I've struggled with too, I must admit."

Really? "In what way?"

"The world at large would paint me as useless because of my malady. I cannot run my own shop without help anymore. I have trouble finishing duties without aching for days. And to pick up my nephew and his wife from the airport, I have to argue for an hour for anyone to believe I'm up to the task."

Didn't this woman know how amazing she was? "And yet, you find time to encourage everyone you come in contact with. You pray for them." Or so Ginny and Sophia had told her. "*That* is not useless."

"But what is useful about loving others well if it doesn't produce results?"

"What results matter more than making someone feel loved or loving in return?"

"What results indeed?" A twinkle lit in Mavis's eyes, reflecting the lights overhead.

Ah . . . "I think I understand what you're saying.

But I've told you, I've already given up on trying to make my dad love me."

"But what about God? You say you want to please him—and that is good. Very good. But do you know the thing that pleases him most? Not all the things you do for him or do in his name but *sitting* with him. Enjoying his presence. Loving him. Talking to him."

Mavis squeezed Sarah's hands. "My dear, you do not need to do anything to make God love you more. He already loves you as much as he possibly can simply because he made you and you are his daughter. And as such, he wants you to enjoy the good things he gives you. Good things, perhaps, like the love of a good man."

Now Mavis had done it. The tears threatening to fall whooshed down Sarah's cheeks. She couldn't remember the last time she'd cried so much in one week. "But why? Why would he love me like that after how I've disappointed him? All the times I turned away when I should have run to him? All the times I behaved in a shameful way that wasn't what he would want for me?"

"Why?" Mavis cupped Sarah's chin as a grand-mother might. "Because he's a good father. He's a good God. And his sacrifice is enough to cover all of our imperfections."

Sarah couldn't help it. She leaned forward and hugged Mavis, whose sugar and flour scent brought scenes from Ginny's bakery to mind. "I don't know what to do."

Mavis feathered a kiss across Sarah's temple where a headache had started forming moments before. "You don't but he does. Seek God's wisdom. And in the meantime, stop concerning yourself with what everyone else would have you do, even yourself."

CHAPTER 15

"The final flight to London Heathrow tonight will begin boarding in one-half hour." Despite the late time, the gate agent's peppy voice flowed from the speakers through the departure lounge.

All around them, people gathered in seats, on the floor, against the walls, some sleeping, some watching movies on their devices. Her soon-to-be-fellow passengers snagged last-minute coffee and cocoa from the small cafe and packaged snacks from the gift shop. A mom across the room fed tiny cheese crackers to her messy-mouthed toddler while a baby slept in the stroller next to her. Down the row of chairs, a woman spoke into her phone in a language that sounded Slavic in nature. Someone nearby smelled as if they hadn't worn deodorant in years.

"Do you need anything else before we board?"

Warren set his iPad on his lap. He'd spent the last hour working while Sarah had pretended to read her own emails. Melissa had sent a slew in the last few days, and Sarah needed to catch up. But not even New Dawn work could distract her from the fraying edges of her heart.

"I'm good. Thanks." Sarah diverted her attention to her phone.

"Sarah."

"Hmmm?" When she peeked back up at him, he wore a grim expression.

The iPad was shoved into his laptop bag, and he crossed his arms over his chest. "I know you don't have to tell me this, but I've been wondering about something. What was in that letter your dad asked me to deliver to you?"

"Oh, that. Nothing." She shrugged and once again looked at her email, swiping her screen for good measure.

But her efforts to make it seem as if she were busy proved fruitless. With a light touch, Warren tugged the phone from her hand and set it inside her purse.

She sighed and twisted her studded earring. "He pulled out all his tricks to try to get me to come home."

"Like . . ."

She pursed her lips. After all, as nice as Warren was, he was part of the Boston business community, part of her parents' world. And as her mother had frequently reminded her as a child, *family laundry should never be aired in front of others.*

"Oh, come on, Sarah. Forgive me for saying so but everyone knows your dad is a bully."

Her eyes widened of their own accord before she could control them. "But he seems to have so many friends."

"Ever heard the term 'frenemies?' It's childish, I know, but it seems to suit." He tilted his head. "People aren't dumb. They hold your father close enough to benefit from his acquaintance, but no one really trusts him."

"But your father is thinking of going into business with him."

"Yes, but as you may remember, when it comes to business, my father is also someone who does what is best for himself."

"So . . ." She gestured between the two of them. "You and I dating or not dating . . ."

"Won't affect his decision to merge companies with your father's in any way."

Sarah slumped in her chair, her shoulders lightened. "I'm so glad to hear that."

"I'm sorry that you felt pressured to date me at all."

She straightened at the hurt pervading his words. "No, Warren, that's not it. I've told you I think you're wonderful."

"I know. But someone else has captured your heart."

"Yes."

"Yet here you are."

"Yes." Her nose tingled. Oh goodness. No more tears. She couldn't take it.

"So"—Warren leaned closer—"what exactly was in that letter?"

Rubbing her eyes, Sarah considered his request. Oh, forget what Mother always said. The fact was, Sarah trusted Warren. He was a friend, and even though she'd hurt him, she prayed they could remain so. Goodness knew she'd need friends when heading back to the wolves. She leaned over, snagged an envelope from her bag, lifted the crumpled paper from inside, and shoved it into Warren's hands. "Read it for yourself."

"Are you sure?"

"Yes."

While he read, she watched as his face turned steadily redder. The paper lowered from his hands in slow unease. "I hope you'll forgive me for what I'm about to do." He stood, walked to the trash can, and tossed the letter inside.

A staccato laugh pulsed from her throat. "Why did you do that?"

Warren sat again. "That's where it belonged." Tapping the metal arm of his seat, Warren studied her. "Sarah, I've already told you that people in our circles think of your dad as a bully. But I would be remiss if I didn't tell you what they think of you."

"Oh, I don't—"

"You need to know this. Despite that you're George Bentley's daughter, you are well respected. And do you know why?"

"Because I work hard?"

"That's important, sure, but we all work hard." Warren's fingers stilled. "People like dealing with you. You're honest and trustworthy and impress people just because you're you. You don't have to be or do anything else. Being Sarah Bentley is enough."

Was that really true—for people and for God?

Yes. The answer resonated deeply in her soul.

But where did that leave her? More self-assured, maybe, but how did she move forward differently? Changed?

Mavis's words from earlier this evening flew back to her mind: *"Seek out God's wisdom. And in the meantime, stop concerning yourself with what everyone else would have you do, even yourself."*

OK then.

She squeezed Warren's hand. "Thank you."

"You're welcome. And one more thing."

Sarah arched an eyebrow. "What?"

"Like your father, I know Jeff Gentry. He's a terrible man, and I'm not surprised that he may be abusing his wife." He sat up straighter. "I want to support your work at New Dawn. And I'm confident my father will too. His father was abusive to my grandmother, and my dad despises men who aren't kind to their significant others."

"What? Seriously?" Sarah's heart pounded as her brain processed the words he was saying.

"Yes, seriously. And I'm sure we can find many others to donate to such a worthy cause. In fact, I'd love to host a charity ball in New Dawn's honor to raise funds."

And here came the waterworks once more. "Warren Kensington, you are amazing."

A smile flashed across his face. "So I've been told."

"But for real. Thank you." She gave him a hug. "Whoever you end up with will be a lucky woman indeed."

He squeezed her shoulders and then let her go. For a moment, he studied her. "So, what are you going to do now?"

She glanced at the clock behind the gate agent's desk. Only ten minutes until the flight was supposed to board—ten minutes to make a decision that would change her life forever.

But it only took ten seconds.

She reached into her bag, pulled out a notebook, wrote the words "I quit," and ripped the page from the binding. Then she folded the paper and handed it to Warren. "Give this to my dad, will you?"

"Absolutely."

"And would you mind collecting my suitcase in Boston and holding onto it until I get home?"

"Of course not."

"Thanks." Sarah pecked Warren on the cheek. "Merry Christmas, Warren."

"Merry Christmas, Sarah."

Sarah stood, gathered her bags, and raced for the exit.

CHAPTER 16

oday had been magical. Sarah only prayed that this evening would be as well.

From her spot inside the lighthouse, she had watched the sky move from a golden mist to a black velvet blanket sprinkled with stardust. At Ginny's enthusiastic insistence, Steven had helped Sarah lug all the things she'd need for tonight here, a mile outside of the village, on Christmas Eve. She'd given her future brother-in-law a hug and he'd shrugged. He was, he'd said, glad she'd be with them for Christmas after all.

Sarah sat on a cozy quilt, a basket of Ginny's goodies opened and a portable heater going nearby. From her spot next to the windows, the ocean looked like a painting, one that moved and crashed and frolicked. She'd brought a plastic lantern, but the moon's rays spilled inside, providing all the light necessary.

It was perfect.

All that she needed now? Her date.

Sarah picked up her phone once more and woke up the screen. Bright white font flashed that it was 6:08 p.m. He should have been here by now. Maybe he wasn't coming. Still, eight minutes late wasn't really late, was it? Especially when she didn't know for sure that he was free.

He hadn't responded to her texts, after all.

And she'd sent several. In fact, today had been as much about self-reflection as preparing for this date, this chance to woo back Michael and apologize for how she'd treated him. She'd conquered the trepidation of driving on the wrong side of the road and borrowed Ginny's car to go to the gardens where Michael had taken her a week and a half ago. All by herself, she'd snapped photo after photo of the gorgeous greenery.

Sure, the photos were on her phone and not Michael's fancy camera.

But she'd remembered what he'd said that day: *"They're yours, and that makes them perfect. Don't let anyone ever tell you any differently."*

And she wouldn't. Not anymore.

After that she'd gotten back into the car, turned on the heater to warm her numb fingers, and sent him a few of her favorites. No caption. She figured he'd just understand her in that way that he seemed to have.

Next, Sarah had made her way back to Port Willis and visited all the spots of significance to the two of them—the spot on the bluffs above the harbor, Ginny's kitchen, and, of course, the hills outside of Mr. Trengrouse's cottage where she'd first kissed him. Then she'd texted a photo of each one to him.

And at last, she'd sent him a photo from the lighthouse an hour ago, finally attaching a caption: *Would you meet me here, in the place where my heart became yours? I'm waiting.*

Sarah checked her phone again, but the only texts were from her father. She didn't bother to read them, just deleted each one as it came through. Yes, she'd have to deal with him eventually, but he wasn't ruining tonight for her.

And even if Michael didn't show up, she'd be OK. After all, she was loved by the Most High, and nothing would ever change that.

Still . . . she really hoped he'd come.

"Sarah?"

Her neck swiveled toward the stairs where Michael stood, a bewildered look on his face. Dressed in only a sweater and jeans—no gloves covered his reddened fingers, and no coat protected him from the wind—he didn't seem to be anything but unsure, shocked to see her. Wasn't he freezing?

"Hi." Though she longed to throw herself into his arms, she couldn't. Every muscle in her body stiffened from where she sat on the blanket.

"Are you really still here?" Michael took one step toward her then stopped, blinking at a quick pace as if to confirm what was in front of him.

"I am." She lifted her hand toward him. "Join me so I can explain?"

And then he was there, lowering himself to his knees in front of her, his eyes scanning her, drinking her in.

He lifted his hand to her face, and she flinched at his icy touch.

"Sorry."

As he started to pull away, she snatched his fingers between her own and blew into them, her eyes never leaving his. Then, she put his hand back on her cheek and turned her lips into his palm, kissing it. The tips of his fingers dug with a light touch into the roots of her hair near her ear.

Sarah cleared her throat. "No, I'm sorry. I left without explanation. Michael, I was scared, and I'll admit I still am. But I know now, without a doubt, that you were right that day. Real love isn't selfish."

She bit her lip, praying she could remember the words she'd read earlier, the ones she'd been committing to memory all day long. "'And more than that, we don't yet see things clearly. We're squinting in a fog, peering through a mist. But it won't be long before the weather clears and the sun shines brightly! We'll see it all then, see it all as clearly as God sees us, knowing him directly just as he knows us! But for right now, until that completeness, we have three things to do to lead us toward that consummation: Trust steadily in God, hope unswervingly, love extravagantly. And the best of the three is love.'"

"That's one of my favorite passages of Scripture."

"Mine too. Because it speaks just perfectly to where I am right now. The truth is, Michael, I *don't* know exactly how to reconcile this thing between us and my love for my ministry back home. But I don't have to. I just have to keep trusting in the love of my heavenly father, hoping for amazing things . . . and loving with everything I have."

She paused then took a deep breath. "And I do. I love you." Would he think her crazy for saying it? Yes, they'd known each other such a short time, but—

"I love you too, Sarah Bentley. Most extravagantly." The pad of his thumb traced a line down the side of her face until he reached her lips.

"Oh?" The word released from her lungs, a happy sigh, and she angled her face upward.

"Yes, oh." His face split into a smile as he chuckled. "And as for what comes next, I've got a lot of vacation time saved. Perks of working for your parents." He winked. "I think a long visit to Boston may be in order."

"Oh?"

"Is that all you can say?"

Her hands came up and around his neck, resting there as she played with the curls at the base of his neck. "No. There's one more thing I'd like to say to you."

He moved in closer, so only their noses touched. Beyond the glass, she could hear the distant roar of the ocean, as if it approved. "And what's that?"

"What did you think of my photos?"

His guffaw shook them both, and he pulled back ever so slightly. "That's not what I thought you were going to say. But since you asked, I thought they were brilliant. I suppose I'm a bit biased, though."

"Hmmm." A lazy grin spread across her lips. "I find I'm quite all right with that. Now." She tilted her head. "Would you please kiss me already?"

"I thought you'd never ask."

And he complied with her request most thoroughly.

Quick Author's Note

THANK you for joining Sarah and Michael on their journey! I hope you enjoyed it as much as I did.

Want to see Warren get his happily ever after? He deserves it after that grand gesture turned awry, doesn't he? Don't worry, there's a woman who's perfect for him…even if she doesn't know it yet.

You can find their story in Like a Silver Bell. Read on for a sneak peek…

Chapter 3: In which Kara Elise Gentry, who works at New Dawn after her divorce, arrives in Cornwall to help plan a Christmas ball for donors

Jeff might be a lying, abusive jerk, but he was right about one thing—England *was* enchanting at Christmastime.

Kara turned slowly, taking it all in. From her spot, where the Port Willis harbor met the end of High Street, she could see a good chunk of the Cornish village. Dinghies and other small fishing craft bobbed in the waves that were gentled by the rocky quay extending parallel to the land. Adorable wooden storefronts painted in a variety of pastels lined the cobblestone street, piping smoke into Sunday's early evening sky.

She, Sarah, and Sarah's husband, Michael—New Dawn's photographer—had only been in town a few hours, after their long trek had landed them finally at Cornwall Airport Newquay. There, Sarah's in-laws had picked them up and dropped Kara's luggage by Rebecca's, an adorable bed and breakfast taking up residence next to a charming bookstore and bakery combo.

That was the whole town—adorable. And so different from the hustle and bustle and smog of Boston.

Kara couldn't wait to see the manor where the fundraiser would take place. It was several miles outside of town, but if it was anything like the village itself, the pictures wouldn't do it justice.

After the stop at the B&B, Michael's parents had insisted Kara join them for a late lunch at their restaurant, the Village Pub, where she'd had her fill of delicious roasted chicken stew and homemade bread. Sarah's younger sister and brother-in-law, Ginny and Steven Applegate, had joined them, as had Michael's sister and her young family.

It had been a loud, raucous affair, but Kara was glad for some quiet just now.

Though she'd hated to admit how tired she was— lack of sleep plus jet lag would do that to a person— the fact that Kara had nearly fallen asleep in her meal had been a fairly good indicator. A walk would be just what she needed to unwind from the lengthy travel and keep her awake until evening.

She started the jaunt back toward the bed and breakfast, anxious to change into loungewear and curl up with a mug of hot chocolate and a good book. Most of the shops—from an antique store to a grocer to a few restaurants—appeared to be closed. Sarah had mentioned something about Sundays being big family days here. The thought pierced Kara's chest. Her own family was so far away.

Reaching into her purse, she pulled out her phone and dialed Jeff's number for the first of her daily chats with Rose. The phone rang and rang before rolling over to voicemail, and her chest tightened even more. Jeff had better not try to keep Rose from talking with her. They'd agreed.

Not that he kept his word all that often. But still. Kara would go full mama bear on him if he tried to withhold her daughter.

She left Rose a quick, peppy voicemail asking her to call back soon and hung up just as she passed a small park that sat on the bluffs overlooking the ocean. "Wow."

Her feet tugged her forward. On one end of the park was a small playground where a handful of children played. Kara listened to the sound of young laughter, wishing Rose's was among them. What was her daughter doing right now? Was Jeff taking good care of her, or was she hanging out in her room or on the iPad he'd insisted on getting for her even though Kara disapproved?

Shaking free of the thoughts, Kara moved toward a gazebo at the opposite end of the park. Beside it stood a Christmas tree that must have been fifteen or maybe even twenty feet tall. It was decorated with red and silver bulbs and strand after strand of darkened lights. The gazebo roof had also been strung with lights. She imagined it all lit up against the sky —gorgeous, especially if the stars shone out here with any amount of brightness. The clouds would need to clear away first, though.

A sudden gust of wind whipped Kara's hair back from her face and she hurried toward the gazebo, where a ring of wooden benches would allow her to sit in shelter and enjoy the scenery.

She didn't notice someone already sat there until she was nearly inside.

Him.

Kara halted. Oh no. She could almost hear Cindy cackling with glee from across the pond.

But maybe if she backed away slowly, he wouldn't notice her.

No such luck.

The man glanced up from his phone and blinked a few times. "Kara?"

"H-hi, Warren." She swallowed, her throat suddenly dry. "Good to see you."

Warren tucked away his phone and stood. "You too." He wore jeans that likely cost more than she made in a month, a fashionable black trench coat—probably Burberry—and a purple woven scarf that looked both stylish and functional. Though Kara wasn't petite by any means, his solid presence made her feel short. "Did you just get into town?"

She straightened her spine, hoping to appear taller than she was. Not that it mattered what he thought. "Yes, a few hours ago. I'm staying at a bed and breakfast not far from here and thought a walk sounded nice."

Sarah and Michael were bunking with Ginny and Steven, who had also invited Kara along—but she preferred to have her own place to retreat to. Plus, she'd be in and out so much with preparing for the fundraiser and didn't want to disturb anyone.

"Rebecca's? Me too." A smile lit Warren's face. Though he was normally clean-shaven, today a dusting of dark stubble covered his sculpted jaw, lending him a rather rugged appeal.

And why exactly are you noticing that?

Kara bit the inside of her cheek. "Small world."

He chuckled. "Not as small as you'd think. I'm pretty sure this town only has a few places to stay."

"Right." Taking a step backward, Kara forced a smile. "Well, I'd better be getting back there. Work is calling my name."

"I'll join you if you don't mind. I've got hundreds

of emails to comb through myself." In addition to heading up New Dawn's board, he was in charge of the Boston branch of his family's New York-based corporation, which specialized in everything from technology to pharmaceuticals.

Warren stepped forward, and Kara caught a whiff of mandarin orange, black pepper, and lavender. It sent a shiver through her.

Goodness. For the scent of mere cologne to have such an effect on her, she really *was* tired—either that or Cindy's words from two days ago had unfortunately embedded themselves in her brain.

Well, her brain had better get the memo that her heart was trying to send it.

No romance.

Especially not with him.

"Sure. I guess if we're both headed that way." It wasn't as if walking with him signified anything. Besides, he was on the board of directors, which kind of indirectly meant he was one of her bosses, right? She should be polite to her boss.

Kara headed back toward the street.

Following along, Warren inhaled a deep breath and stuck his hands inside the pockets of his coat. "It's nice to be back here."

"You've been to Port Willis before?"

"Once. Three years ago." He glanced at her. "It was actually on that trip that I decided to become part of what New Dawn was doing."

Three years … right about the time she'd decided to leave Jeff.

"Has the town changed much?" Because the last three years had changed everything for her.

"Not really. I think that's what I love about this place—so classically charming, like something out of a painting or kids' storybook. It's why I suggested we hold the fundraiser here instead of London."

As they crossed the street, an old metal lamppost flickered on. Dusk had arrived.

Kara lifted an eyebrow. "That was your idea?" To be honest, when she'd first heard it, she'd thought it a bit of a risk. "How did you know donors would want to travel down here so close to the holidays?" Most of them were not only busy but also lived in London, a four- or five-hour drive from Cornwall.

He shrugged. "I just thought about my ideal holiday and figured others might feel the same way."

Well, that was a mysterious answer. "What's your ideal holiday?" She really didn't want to ask such personal details of him, but it would be good to understand the mindset of the guests who would be attending the fundraiser. After all, if their expectations weren't met, she wouldn't have done her job.

And they wouldn't be likely to donate again.

"Oh, nothing fancy—though I know the ball will be a hit." Warren stepped off the sidewalk onto the street so a family with a stroller could pass. He smiled and nodded a greeting at them before refocusing on Kara. "Mostly, just time away from the craziness of work, a place where I can breathe, where normal life seems a world away."

"You can't get much farther from the norm than here, I suppose." She followed him as he continued around a bend in the road. The bed and breakfast loomed in the distance. "What about planned activities? I have some options for people—daytime sightseeing, tours about the estate grounds, and some nighttime activities in town and at the manor—but I thought most might want to plan their own excursions." She hoped she was right in that regard.

"That sounds great. Our lives are so overplanned already, our calendars so crowded, that I think guests might appreciate some downtime." He chuckled. "Although some might not know what to do with themselves."

"True." She tilted her head, curious about something. "Pardon me for asking, but is that why you're here so much earlier than the other board members?" As far as she knew, they weren't set to arrive until the day before the other donor guests did on Thursday.

Warren nodded. "Sarah invited me to come out early and spend some time with them." He reached for the handle of Rebecca's front door. "Over the last several years, I've become closer with her and Michael than my own family."

Huh. And why was that?

But no. She closed her lips before she could ask the question. She didn't need to know anything more than necessary about this man—however pleasant he was being in this moment.

As he opened the door, a rush of warm air met Kara's cheeks. She inhaled the lovely scent of spiced cake and apple cider, which sat on the sidebar of the smallish dining room to the right of the entryway. A petite woman with dirty blonde hair stood behind a wooden desk—Rebecca Trengrouse, the owner. She gave a gruff wave to Kara and Warren before turning back to her computer screen.

It had been a while since Kara had stayed at a bed and breakfast—the last one had been in the Poconos for her and Jeff's third anniversary—and the first time she'd been at one by herself. But one glance at the cozy living room warmed by a stone fireplace that was flanked by bookcases and an undecorated Christmas tree, and Kara knew she'd found a home away from home.

She'd stay here every night of her trip if she could, but she needed to be on hand at the estate come Thursday and until she flew out next Sunday. Unless she decided to stay longer, like Cindy had suggested when Kara had told her about the change of Christmas plans. Hmm.

Either way, for now, she'd enjoy the peace. The quiet. The warmth.

Kara let loose a contented sigh.

"It's quite charming, isn't it?"

Her hand flew to her chest. Right. Warren was still with her, wasn't he?

"Yes." She grimaced at the sudden coolness in her voice. "I guess I'll see you around."

"It'll be hard not to. I think we're the only guests staying here this week."

Her breathing ratcheted up a notch. "What?"

That couldn't be right. Surely more would be coming in at some point. She'd have to check with Rebecca. Otherwise, how was she supposed to avoid Warren? Kara already didn't like her body's response to him. And with the absence of Rose and the stress of pulling off this event, her mind was in a fragile place.

She could not afford any distractions—even one so handsome as Warren Kensington.

As quick as St. Nick in that Christmas Eve poem her mom had read to her and Cindy as kids, the peace Kara had sensed in this place flew out the charming little B&B window.

Come fall in love with Kara, Warren, and the entire village of Port Willis in Like a Silver Bell, Book 3 in the Port Willis Romance series, available today on your favorite ebook platform.

OR

Save yourself a little money by picking up Port Willis: The Complete Collection box set, which includes all four Port Willis sweet romance novellas.

ABOUT THE AUTHOR

Lindsay Harrel is a lifelong book nerd who lives in Arizona with her young family and two golden retrievers in serious need of training. When she's not writing or chasing after her children, Lindsay enjoys making a fool of herself at Zumba, curling up with anything by Jane Austen, and savoring sour candy one piece at a time.

She also writes sweet romantic comedies (same sweetness, same heat level!) under the pen name Kristin Canary. Check out her books there at kristincanary.com.

9 781961 223301